MONTE JAFFE

The Hole in the Heart

NOVEL

Dear Helen,

Enjoy!

Monte

About the author

Monte Jaffe began writing in Chattanooga, Tennessee, where he was born, composing songs and writing short stories and TV scripts.

He supported the civil rights movement, working and living with the Highlander Folk Group, followers of Martin Luther King.

He later moved to New York, going underground to avoid being drafted into the Vietnam War. He did roofing and construction work and worked as a social worker in the notorious Hell's Kitchen. Echoes of these challenges reverberate through the pages of his novels.

In 1982 he moved to Europe, pursuing a successful career singing opera. Presently he lives with his wife in northern Germany.

Visit him on www.montejaffe.com

There is a light that exists in the clouds which envelop the earth, a light that swirls and dives into the caves of these clouds. This light finds its way into the most hidden, most secret crannies of darkness. A piece of this light has found its way into the flame of a candle burning next to a bed in a bordello in Antwerp.

The room is sparse: a double bed, beside it a small table, some blue material to cover an unpainted wall, a window with the curtain drawn, a sink to wash in between customers, a shelf for condoms and oils, a small refrigerator for beer or champagne, for a price. Everything fits the atmosphere of sex by agreement. Time is money, nothing extra, nothing overly fancy, nothing except the burning candle. The prostitute is a 'window girl', with olive skin and long black hair, still young. On the bed is the client, Sam. He's in his mid-fifties, with a scar on his back under the left shoulder and a concentration camp number tattooed on his arm. They are finished. She puts on her panties and bra, he puts on his pants. The prostitute glances at the tattoo.

"Why don't you get rid of that? They can take those things off."

Sam answers gruffly.

"Don't worry about it."

"I'm sorry, I'm... "

"Don't worry about it. It's a phone number I don't want to forget."

"Yeah, hey, next Friday, right? Same time?"

"Next Friday, six-thirty. Be well."

Sam leaves through the door to the street. The prostitute blows out the candle, opens the curtain and retakes her position in the chair in the window.

Among the sane of us there is a signal in our mind that tells us that we are here and this is now. This signal retains a linear present throughout our time of living. The past is over except in our memory, the present is the thing we are doing and the future is the future. Among the insane of us, the signal is very flexible. The now is yesterday and the yesterday is now and there is no future. Sam's mind belongs to the second category. He is freed from the prison of a now that fits in a package of time that is over when it begins. Perhaps now is now and perhaps now is yesterday. The price for this freedom is high. Don't ask to pay it. But if you have the dark privilege of having paid, then let your nows swim, and swim with yourself.

Sam leaves the bordello. He walks past the window and down the street. The now signal in his mind slips. His now becomes dawn, April 1945. Sam is now a skeleton wearing a filthy prisoner's uniform. He is stumbling through ice-cold rain somewhere near Dachau. He and a stream of half-living human beings are being herded through villages by German soldiers, herded to a substation near Dachau, but

Sam doesn't know where he is, only that he must keep moving. If he stops, he will be shot. He hears the plodding feet of those behind him and in front of him. He hears his breath.

Somewhere in front of Sam is his son Yitzchak. Sam and Yitzchak had tried to stay together but Sam is weak. He fell behind. The soldiers pushed Yitzchak forward. The rain is mixed with pieces of ice. Knife blades of ice cut Sam's face as he walks. He tries to keep his eyes open, tries to find his son somewhere in the staggering herd of human beings in front of him. One back looks like another. One stumbling plod looks like another. The soldiers walk with the prisoners, keeping a careful watch for any signs of lagging, any signs of slowing down. That was the first signal, lagging, slowing down. Then came dropping what they were carrying, then stopping, standing. Then they had to be shot. That happened often. The ditches alongside the road were filled with blood and rain.

Suddenly the air screams. Huge black planes come out of the sky. The Allied Forces mistake the marching column of prisoners for Wehrmacht. Bombs fall a few hundred meters from the column of walking skeletons. Fighter planes strafe the road. Prisoners and German soldiers fall to the ground. Some are hit. Some are taking cover. German soldiers fire in all directions. Sam hears someone shout, "Run. Run for it!" The prisoners run toward the forest. The Germans fire at the escaping prisoners. Most are killed. Complete chaos breaks out. Shouting and the deafening roar of the fighter planes split the air. Sam stops walking and stares in front of him. About fifty meters away, he sees Yitzchak standing, looking at him. Sam walks toward Yitzchak, oblivious to the bleeding bodies around him, oblivious to the bombs and machinegun fire. Sam reaches Yitzchak. He stretches his arms out and embraces his son. A German soldier gets up on one knee and aims his rifle at Sam. He fires. The bullet enters Sam's back near his shoulder. Sam and Yitzchak fall unconscious into the puddles of blood and mud. The soldier walks over to Sam and Yitzchak. He aims his rifle at Sam's head. A fighter plane pours its ammunition into the face and chest of the German soldier.

After many hours the noise stops. The planes fly away. The German soldiers and what is left of the prisoners move on. The dead lay staring at the oncoming black night. There are no stars, no moon. Yitzchak opens his eyes and sees nothing. He thinks he is blind. He staggers to his feet. With his hands out in front of him, like a blind drunk, he makes his way over the corpses and into the black void.

The next day Sam wakes up with his mouth and nose full of mud and ice. He is lying face down. His shoulder burns. He rolls over onto his back. He doesn't have the strength to spit the filth out of his mouth. Sam makes a choking sound, "Yitzchak". Then he passes out. When he wakes up, the sun is high in the sky. It shines like a policeman's flashlight in his face. He jerks up, not wanting to be kicked by a German soldier, kicked to get up and start walking. Sam gets to his feet. He is the first up. Everyone else is sleeping or dead. Sam stumbles down the road, wondering when the others will join him, wondering how far ahead Yitzchak is or if Yitzchak is still sleeping or if Yitzchak is one of the bodies he is stumbling over. Sam walks on, wondering if he is going in the right direction.

Morning. Quiet. There is a lead-tasting stillness in the air. Three soldiers, looking like black bugs, cautiously come out of the forest next to a barn. Then fifty more soldiers appear, following them like black blood drops, trickling horizontally towards the farm. The soldiers are American. A sergeant indicates to a private to check out the barn and moves on. The private enters the barn with extreme caution, rifle at ready. It is warm in the barn, clean. The private moves past stalls containing a horse, a cow. The soldier hears a sound behind him. He spins around, ready to kill. In an empty stall behind him, curled in a pile of hay, he sees an emaciated boy wearing a ragged striped uniform. The soldier kneels next to the boy. The boy cringes. The private whispers,

    "It's OK, it's OK."

The private takes off his coat and gently wraps it around the boy. Slowly Yitzchak crawls into the private's arms. The two sit in the stall, gently rocking back and forth. The horse and the other animals watch this event. One is reminded of another manger.

##############

After a war, the living regroup in new combinations. The love that bound them to the people they lost binds them now to new mothers, fathers, sons, daughters, friends. Death leaves the field and Time embraces even the ruined and gives Life back its natural triumph.

Yitzchak is now twelve years old. He has been adopted by a family in Antwerp, a religious family with its own dark history. His new father is a cantor in the neighborhood synagogue. He and Yitzchak are sitting under a tree outside the synagogue. The cantor is teaching Yitzchak to become a cantor, to lead the Shabbos Service. Without being aware of it, Yitzchak pulls a leaf from the tree. The cantor cautions Yitzchak.

"Yitzchak, today is Shabbos. You shouldn't take a leaf from the tree."

"Why not? It's just a leaf."

"When you take the leaf from a tree, it kills the leaf. It's like taking a child from its family."

Yitzchak looks at the leaf in his hand.

"I was taken from my family and I didn't die."

"Baruch Shem (Thank God)"

"You see, we leaves are not so fragile."

"Some leaves are and some aren't."

"I'm a strong leaf."

"Baruch Shem."

Yitzchak gently puts the leaf on the ground.

"Why are some people strong and some not? Was my father strong?"

"He was very strong. To have a son like you, he must have been a giant of a man, a soul as strong as a lion."

"I remember him holding me.. He held me very tight, then we fell. That's all I can remember. My mother was strong, too. She used to sing to me. Her voice was very low. I will be Bar Mitzvah in a few weeks. I will be a man. I will be a tree like that one (he points to a small tree). Not a big tree, but I won't be a leaf any more. Do you believe in God?"

" Do you?"

"It's Shabbos. I must be honest. "

"Be honest."

"If there were a God with a long white beard, would all those horrible things… There is no God. God is an invention in the Torah."

"For me God is a feeling, God is a warm feeling that holds the world together."

"But God doesn't make sense."

"No, Yitzchak. God doesn't make sense. Maybe it's not important that God makes sense."

Yitzchak looks seriously into the cantor's face.

"But things have to make sense. I will soon be a man and I want to know what I'm supposed to do. My father would want me to find his killer and to kill him. My mother, too. I can't just do nothing. Not as a man. As a boy I could – but not as a man."

The cantor gently takes the boy's face in his hands.

"In a few weeks, you will give your Bar Mitzvah. There will be many people listening to you, many people who have memories like you. Many who could take a gun in their hand instead of a siddur. But every prayer that you sing, every law, every rule in our religion has one purpose and only one purpose, to show the highest respect and love for life. If we don't love life, then what is the tragedy of a loss of life? You are young, maybe one day your questions will be answered. But I think I know what your mother and your father really would want. They would want you to leave death behind. They would want you to live, to receive the love they wanted to give you. To receive love and then to give love, that's our purpose in life. That's the order we yearn for. And there is one more thing I must tell you, one more thing I want you to know. I love you, Yitzchak, I love you."

The cantor puts his arms around Yitzchak.

A few weeks later, Yitzchak is standing at the bima. He is dressed in a white silk robe with a white silk yarmulke. He is alone on the bima and he faces towards the Ark. He is about to begin his Bar Mitzva. He glances over his shoulder to see the cantor standing with the congregation. Yitzchak feels his father's arms holding him for a last suspended moment, then he remembers falling into empty space. Yitzchak turns to the Ark and sings,

"Shochen ad moro vkodesh shmo."

The congregation answers and the Shabbos service has begun.

###############

After the war, when enough pieces of Sam's life were put together so that he could function, Sam took refuge in theatre. He wrote plays, plays about humans and inhumanness. He is in a theatre in Jaffa, Israel. The theatre seats about two hundred. Three actors are rehearsing WAITING FOR GODOT – in Arabic. Adib is the play's director and also the director of the Jaffa Theater. Sam's latest play will be premiered at the Jaffa Theater and Adib will direct it. Sam smiles at the spectacle in front of him, Beckett in Arabic. He jokes.

       "Beckett would love this." Adib smiles,

       "I love this." He speaks to the Beckett cast.

       "OK, that's good. Take ten and set up for REAL ESTATE. I want to work with some costumes today. I need a smoke break."

       Sam and Adib are standing outside the theatre entrance. The theatre is part of a larger building built in the old city's style. Behind them is a sign advertising coming plays. The sign reads: JAFFA THEATER presents double bill: WAITING FOR GODOT by Samuel Beckett and REAL ESTATE by Samuel Levine. Premiere Thursday March 28, 8 PM.

Sam lights Adib's cigarette, then his own.

"I understand Beckett's play in Arabic better than I do in English."

"I didn't know you spoke Arabic."

Sam smiles.

"I don't."

Adib looks down the hill at a stately house, the oriental version of a mansion, but in disrepair.

"My father used to own that house, and his father before him. Many Arabs used to live in this area. You can't touch anything here for under a million dollars, and if you're an Arab, you can't touch it, period."

"Times change, Adib."

"That's easy to say, Sam. That's easy to say."

"Is it?"

"You're a cynical son of a bitch, Sam."

"Why, because I don't listen to all this bullshit about your history? Do you listen to my history? Does anyone listen to anyone's history? We're killing each other. Do we ask why? What's causing it? No, we just continue the killing spiral. You break my heart. I break yours. I am tired of holding everyone's lies in my arms. What's really in your heart, Adib? You want that fucking mansion. You want to throw the bastards out. Kick them out. Sit your ass in your living-room. Then what? Then you're sitting in your living-room and the walls are painted with blood and we're all sitting on piles of bodies, watching slaughter on TV, screaming, 'Mine, mine, this real estate is mine'."

"We're not all victims. You're paranoid, Sam. We are not living in the Third Reich. You should settle down, Sam. Anger is good for writing plays, but of no use when the play is over and you want to go home. Where do you go, Sam?"

"Don't worry. I go, I go."

"Where? To your wife? To your children? To your friends? Where? You need a woman, a family. Everyone does."

"I have a wife. Do you think those impotent weapons really kill? Do you think little bullets have that power? Adib, I'm happy you think that. I'm happy for you because it means you don't have horror in your every conscious moment. I have a wife. I have a child. My wife is beautiful. That is why they separated her from the other women. They put her with the beautiful women. They made her fuck. They put her in the special barracks and made her fuck. Then they shot her. But I swear by the old almighty monster you call God, they did not kill her. They did not touch her, because she is here in my chest. Rachel and my son are in my chest. Look! (He pulls his shirt off). See this scar, the little bullet missed my chest. They crawled into my chest and they live there. They are safer in my chest than all those fools in living-rooms. You say I'm cynical, Adib, I'm not cynical – I'm infected. Death and life are the same to me. People who die are alive forever. I'm just waiting to quit dying. That's not cynical, Adib, I won't give the bastards the satisfaction of making me cynical. After the rehearsal I have to catch a plane. I have to get back to Antwerp. I have to see my wife. She keeps the Shabbos. She lights the candles. I have to get back."

Sam goes back into the theatre and sits in a dark corner, in the back of the house. Adib is standing with his assistant, near the stage, watching it being set up for Sam's play. The set is two wooden beds with a partition separating them, a door stage right. The actors come onto the stage. A young woman in a robe is on the arm of a German soldier. Another beautiful young woman, Tagrit, is sitting on one of the beds. She is wearing a concentration camp jacket over normal blue jeans. She has long beautiful hair. Adib sits in the house and calls out to the REAL ESTATE cast.

"OK, when you're ready."

A couple walk across the stage toward the unoccupied bed. Adib calls to the actress Tagrit.

"Tagrit." He motions to her arm. Tagrit answers.

"It's a rehearsal, Adib. It's hard to wash the ink off."

Adib motions again and sends his assistant up to the stage who writes a number on Tagrit's arm and returns. Tagrit mumbles, "OK, OK." Adib starts again. "From the top."

The couple walk again across the stage and sit on their bed. In comes a German officer. He looks at Tagrit.

"Hello, you're new."

He takes off his jacket and stands next to Tagrit.

"What's your name?"

Tagrit reacts terrified, huddled on the bed. She doesn't answer.

"What's your name? You have a name."

The actress responds softly.

"Rachel." She says the name in the Hebrew accent.

"What?"

"Rachel."

"Rachel, ah, Rachel. Let me see you, Rachel."

He stands in front of Tagrit and unbuttons his pants.

"Take your clothes off. Come, undress. I said, take your clothes off!"

Slowly, Rachel takes off her jacket.

"Here, my dear, open. I said open! Don't you know how to do it? I said, open!"

(He slaps Rachel across the face.)

"Do it right. There. Yeah, yeah, yeah, that's better. Good. Good."

Sam watches from the dark corner in the auditorium. Why? Why does he watch his wife being tortured? Why did he even bring the horrible memory into life by writing it? Is it masochism? Is it the sick behavior of a tormented victim of the Holocaust? Or is it an act of love? Is it his attempt to ease her pain by sharing it with her? For better and for worse. Is it his reaching to her to say, 'You are not alone, my love. I share your shame and I am by you. We will live together even in shame and in death.'

The premiere is going well. The audience, many of whom could have added their own personal memories to the evening, has witnessed humans being humane and inhumane. There remains only the final speech. Tagrit, the actress playing Rachel, stands center stage, the last of a long line of men, women, children, all in concentration camp uniforms, about forty extras crowded onto the stage. They all stand with their backs to the audience, facing a large door over which hangs a sign reading: 'SHOWER'.

The style of the staging is not realistic but symbolic, Brechtian-like.

Tagrit wears a concentration camp uniform. Her long beautiful hair has now been shorn. She turns and speaks directly to the play's audience.

"Well, dear audience, it's time for me to take the famous shower. You've seen it many times, I'm sure, people screaming, crying. Maybe you'll be able to make my voice out. You know my voice by now. You've been hearing it all night. Maybe you'll say 'Oh my God, that's Rachel'. But then probably not. I think I'll scream in a new way, a way I've never screamed before and never will again. Or is that true? Have I screamed like that before? What do we have now? 1974. I think I screamed in 1840. I was what the Americans call an 'Indian' then. They had the Indian Removal Act. It was another real estate war. Of course, no showers, no running water. Blood ran. 1940 we don't need to talk about. What about 2040? Will I scream again in 2040? Will you hear me scream in 2040? Some of you might. Some of you might be screaming with me. Or will the Messiah come? Now that's of course a nice thought. He will come and there will be no need for plays like this one. Excuse me for breaking the illusion. This is a play. No-one is really dying. Mothers are not burying their children. No-one is really changing from the human wonder into a pile of slime and blood and entrails. We, the intellectuals, wouldn't allow that, would we? Did we? Will we? Well, my friends, back into character. I, Rachel, am about to die. That gives me the freedom to mention a few things. You are all idiots. You are all land-claiming idiots.

Real estate idiots. You won't claim the land, ever. The land will claim you. And as for the Messiah, this earth you want to claim is the Messiah. You are not waiting for her. She is waiting for you. Count on it. Well, it's time. Please excuse me. It's been a lovely evening."

Tagrit turns upstage and joins the group going through the shower door as the curtain falls.

Sam's Real Estate play was successful and was later presented at the Habima, Israel's largest theater and then later as part of the Jerusalem Festival. He and Adib, the play's director, were invited to talk shows where they were required to consolidate the 'message' of the play between commercials. Sam and Adib arrived at the TV studio an hour or so before the broadcast and were required to put on make-up. They had a dressing-room which was equipped with various fruit juices and a lounging-couch and mirrors. The TV station recommended that they wear blue shirts because blue looked good on TV. Sam and Adib were brought from their dressing-rooms to the set, comfortable chairs on a slightly elevated platform, which was surrounded with variations of very important-looking instruments that very accurately threw light. Sam and Adib were seated by assistants, who then returned to their positions behind television cameras, which were rolled around by casually-dressed men with headsets. The studio was very well air-conditioned, the temperature was invigorating. A man wearing a headset held up five fingers, then four, then three, then two, then pointed to the moderator who suddenly smiled and said,

"Boker tov, good morning and welcome to Israel on Stage. We have with us today the playwright, Sam Levine, and director, Adib Phazad. Mr. Levine's play, Real Estate, opened last week at the Habima and Mr. Levine and the play's director, Adib Phazad, have graciously taken time to be here and share their thoughts with us. Good morning, Mr. Levine and Mr. Phazad."

Both Sam and Adib mumble 'good morning'.

"Mr. Levine, what inspired you to write Real Estate?"

"I don't know."

The moderator continued.

"World peace is a theme, yes, even a dream which dominates our daily lives. Your play expresses this dream. Do you have plans for a new work?"

"I don't plan anything. I... I don't plan. Only what happens happens, then I adjust... if I can. I say or write what happened. The question for me is not what I plan, but why do things happen, good or bad? I just ask that question."

The moderator nods.

"Jewish and Arabic relations have been very tense lately. Mr. Phazad, you are an Israeli Arab. What was it like directing this play? Do you think it portrays the Arabic community correctly?"

"There are many different points of view in the Arabic community, even many different communities within the Arabic community. Sam and I have known each other for several years. We're in the same community, so to speak. I don't understand the question. Which community?"

"I mean political community."

"Politicians are all in the same community. The play doesn't deal with political issues. It deals with tragic stupidity and with our future. It asks the audience if we want to repeat our past or if we want to take humanity in a new direction, maybe one without politicians."

"Mr. Levine, do you agree with this analysis?"

"I... I don't analyse. Directors analyse. I write or try to write even when it's hard to write. I let Adib worry about concepts."

"What do you mean, hard to write?"

"I mean the aloneness."

"Mr. Levine, many citizens of Israel are survivors. What does your play say about survivors of the Holocaust?"

"It says that some didn't survive."

The moderator looks into the camera.

"We have to take a commercial break. We'll be right back. Stay with us."

The technical director in the studio booth runs a tape selling Toyota, the car of the future. The floor assistant holds up five fingers and the countdown is repeated. The moderator smiles.

"We're back with Mr. Sam Levine and Mr. Adib Phazad. Mr. Phazad,... "

Sam interrupts.

"What did you do just now?"

The moderator is thrown off, but that's all right. He likes the spontaneous question.

"Do?"

"Just now, we were talking about survivors and you stopped."

"We went to a commercial."

"We were talking about people who lived through the Holocaust and you went to a commercial?"

"Just a short break. We're back now."

"We're back now? Do you see this?" Sam shows the number tattooed on his arm. The technical director asks for a close up of Sam's arm.

Sam continues.

"We're back now? We're fucking back now?"

"Mr. Levine, we went to a commercial."

"Is THIS a commercial?" indicating his arm. "Is this a fucking commercial?"

"Mr. Levine, commercials are a reality. It's what makes television possible."

"You're right. We're back."

Sam got up and left the studio.

############

Sam is in the bordello in Antwerp. He is fully clothed and is looking tenderly toward his prostitute friend. She, on the other hand, is completely naked and in a feisty mood. Sam goes to her. He takes a piece of cloth and gently drapes it over her head. He speaks softly.

"Light the candle."

She takes a Bic lighter and lights the candle next to the bed. She looks into the light. A peacefulness comes into her face, a beauty. Slowly, tenderly, Sam turns her around and gently kisses her. She smiles.

"You're a nice guy. You wanna beer, wine?"

"Yeah, I'll have some wine."

She gets up, puts a robe on and gets him a glass of wine. Sam says,

"Take one for yourself."

"Thanks. What... Whadya do? I can't guess what ya do."

"Go ahead, guess."

"I can't. Hmm... teacher? I don't know."

"I'm a writer."

"A writer? Like... movies? Do you write movies?"

"Sometimes."

"Hey, man, no shit? Movies. Are you in show business? What movies have you written? Have I seen some? What kinda movies? Like... what... murder movies?"

"Yes".

"You write murder movies? Holy shit! Like prostitutes getting murdered? You know, prostitutes get murdered all the time."

"Yes, I write about a prostitute getting murdered."

"Listen, do you need... I mean... if you need... like, I act. I'm a natural born actress. God knows, I act all day long. Look, if you need someone for your movies, maybe we could work something out. Really. Hey, I can sing too."

She starts to sing and dance. Sam starts to leave.

"Wait, watch this."

She breaks into a number.

Sam gets the hell out of there.

"Be well." He leaves.

Sam goes down the street and it begins to rain, a sudden shower that goes berserk. Sheets of rain descend. People run for shelter. Sam, annoyed, looks up at the sky and sees planes flying low over the city. Bombs are falling. The rain continues. People are running to save their lives. Sam is standing absolutely still. Drenched in rain and bombs. He looks across the street and sees another still figure, a young teenager. The teenager is looking at Sam. His face shows a profound disappointment.

"Why, Papa, why didn't you protect me?"

The two figures – Sam and the teenager – are about 50 meters apart, looking at each other. Around them is chaos, chaos racing in the street. People running, rain attacking everything that moves. Only the man and boy are still and oblivious to everything except each other. Sam crosses the street towards the teenager. Cars narrowly miss hitting him. He stands in front of the teenager. Suddenly the teenager's mother runs over and grabs him. They walk away. Sam stands staring at the space where the teenager was. Sam turns and sees a small restaurant with a sign over the door: 'Eden Bar & Grill'. He walks over to the restaurant as the rain continues. He remains unaware of the rain. He stands in front of the plate glass window of the restaurant and peers inside. He sees himself in a room as a young man with Rachel and Yitzchak. They are in their living-room of many years ago. The young Sam is playing with the young Yitzchak and Rachel is watching. She hears a knock on the door in the back of the room. She opens the door. Three men with weapons walk in and shove the family through the door. The living-room is empty. Sam stares through the plate glass window at the empty room – empty of people – but filled with people's things, his things, books, toys, glasses, etc. Using his head as battering-ram, he breaks the window and enters the restaurant. The restaurant is filled with people who have gotten out of the rain. They react. The chaos of the rain and the crowd cover Sam's retreat back into reality. He runs down the street, becoming one of millions of runners.

###############

It's about eight o'clock at night – in Hell's Kitchen in New York. Late fall. Dark. A little boy about ten is starting to cross 53rd Street between a parked pick-up truck and a car. The boy is a black boy, a street boy. His name is Jimmy. A heavy man is sitting in the driver's seat in the pick-up truck. He starts the engine and shouts.

"Hey you little nigger! Get out of the way." Jimmy looks up at the man, picks up a loose rock from the street and throws it at the man. The rock breaks the side window. The heavy man leaps out of the truck and runs after the boy who runs into the tenement building and up the stairs onto the roof. The heavy man runs after him, but not nearly as fast. Jimmy finds some loose bricks on the roof and looks over the side of the roof to find the truck. He sees it and throws the bricks onto the truck, destroying the top of the truck. The heavy man comes onto the roof and tries to grab the boy who dodges him. Jimmy pushes a door and cuts his hand on a piece of sheet metal and runs down the stairs and disappears into the street. The heavy man loses him. Jimmy runs into the Police Athletic League Center on 51st and 10th Avenue. The center is filled with teenagers from around ten years to twenty years old. Boys, girls, all colors and sizes, playing pool, talking, playing ping-pong etc. Jimmy runs into an office. In the office is a young man about thirty, sitting behind the desk. His sleeves are rolled up. He has a number tattooed on his arm. It is Yitzchak.

"Hey Jimmy, what happened?"

"Fucking asshole chasing me!"

"What happened? Let me see your hand. Come here, Jimmy!"

"Son of a bitch."

"Let me see your hand. Man, you got a bad cut there. Let's see it."

He takes out first aid equipment and bandages and cleans the boy's hand. Jimmy bravely suffers the disinfectant.

"I fucking destroyed the bastard's truck. Man, he was pissed off."

"Jimmy, you got a bad cut. You're gonna need a butterfly stitch."

"What the fuck is that?"

"They gonna have to stitch your hand, Jimmy."

"The hell they are. I'm getting out of here." Yitzchak grabs him as he tries to run out.

"Jimmy, cool out man, you got a bad cut. Cool out."

"Hey, listen, Numbers, ain't nobody gonna sew me."

A man sticks his head into the office.

"Izzy, you got a call on three. I think it's from overseas."

40

"Got it." He picks up the phone, holding Jimmy. "Just cool it, Jimmy. (Then into the phone) Mom, it's great to hear you. Everything all right? Mom, you got me at a bad time. Can I call you back? Right, call you later."

"Was that your mom? Hey, Numbers, you told me you didn't have a mom."

"That was my step-mother. Look, we've got to get you to a hospital."

"She live around here? In the neighborhood?"

"My step-family lives in Belgium, in Europe, a town called Antwerp."

"What are you doing here, if your family lives in... what did you say?"

"Antwerp."

"Right, Antwerp. What you doing here if your mother lives in Antwerp?"

"I'll tell you the story of my life later. Let's get this here fixed up."

Jimmy starts to go again.

"My ass. I ain't goin' to no hospital."

Yitzchak grabs him.

"You want to lose your hand? You want to lose your hand, man? I mean this is dangerous shit. They might cut your hand off, if we don't get this thing sewed up."

"You shittin' me?"

"Do I sound like I'm shittin' you? Let's go."

They go out the door and onto the street.

"Jimmy, we'll go to St. Antoine's. Hey Jimmy, don't say fuck so much."

They quickly walk around the corner to St. Antoine's Hospital. They enter the emergency room filled with people waiting. They go to the admission desk. Yitzchak speaks to the man at the desk.

"I'm from the P.A.L. and this young man has cut his hand. He needs a butterfly stitch, I think."

The deskman doesn't look up from his desk.

"Fill this out, please. Are his parents here?"

"He doesn't have any parents."

"Someone from his family has to sign this."

"The boy doesn't have any family. Please just stitch him up."

"I'm sorry, we can't administer to him without family consent."

Yitzchak hits the desk with his fist.

"Cut the shit, just stitch him up."

The desk man looks up with a face that was better when he was looking down.

"I'm sorry. We can't."

Yitzchak and Jimmy turn around and leave the building.

"Don't worry, Jimmy, there are other hospitals."

There are a lot of hospitals in New York. That should tell you something. They go in the emergency entrance of St. James' Hospital, again a waiting-room filled with a large variety of emergencies. They go to the admissions desk.

"Hello, I'm Izzy Levine from the P.A.L., and my friend here needs his hand stitched."

Again a deskman type.

"Please fill out this form. We will need family consent."

"I'll sign."

"Are you a member of his family?"

"I'm his fucking uncle!"

Jimmy smiles.

"Hey, Numbers, you shouldn't say fuck so much."

44

When Yitzchak was a child, an American soldier found him in a pile of hay. The soldier brought Yitzchak to safety and then disappeared from Yitzchak's life. When he was old enough, Yitzchak came to America, maybe not to find the soldier, but to find America and to find himself. He studied Art and painted many pictures. He became skillful. He looked for himself in his paintings. He found Picasso, he found Modigliani, even Jasper Johns. Where am I? America, where am I?

###############

It is about 7:30 a.m., sunrise, lower East Side. A big loft, paintings, canvases everywhere, a big bed at the end of the loft near an improvised kitchen. The loft has space and light. Yitzchak is in blue jeans, no shirt. He is wearing a yarmulke and is putting on his tefillin. Behind him in the bed is his wife, Stacy, who is beginning to stir. She gets out of bed wearing a T-shirt, goes past Yitzchak into the bathroom. Stacy is a black woman.

"Mom called last night," she says, coming out of the bathroom, "and wants to know if we are coming for Chanukah. The show will be running, I don't know if I will be free. Do you want to go?"

"We'll see. When did she call? What time?"

"About eight o'clock."

"It must have been like two or three in the morning there. Insomnia again. After about twenty years

46

things begin to loosen up in the mind, frozen things begin to thaw. I guess that's what keeps her up."

"What about you, my love? Will you, what did you call it, thaw?"

"I've got you, my love. So, if it comes, it comes."

"Do you want to do some work? I'll make some coffee. Do you want me to pose?"

"No, I don't want you to pose. I just want you."

Yitzchak takes Stacy in his arms and they draw each other to bed.

Late fall in New York is a serious time of year. It's an urgent time. The wind comes off the Hudson as if it has some place to go, none of this lazy summer breeze. Loving someone in the fall is a good idea. It's a good way to stay

47

warm. Yitzchak and Stacy are keeping each other warm as they walk along the Hudson.

"Izzy, my love, it's great to have my own private Jew."

"If I had stayed in Antwerp, my wife might be wearing a wig."

"Oyi yoi yoi!"

"I wish you could have met my real mother and father. I wish they could have known you."

"What would they think? Be honest!"

"Who knows? Before the war they might have been afraid; after, what's to be afraid of? I think that if anything is holy on this planet, it's the earth. If anything is wise, if anything loves, it's earth. Earth loves. We are supposed to be made of it. It takes us into its family when we are finished. It takes all of us, accepts all of us and everything about us. No conditions. That's the way I see my parents. They would love you like the earth loves."

"Where do you get these ideas, Izzy?"

"They come to me from Ethiopia. My love, all good things come from Ethiopia. It's good to have my private Ethiopian."

A painter has to make a living. It's only after the painter is dead that he or she is rich. It's Yitzchak's working with children at the Police Athletic League that keeps him in colors. He is talking with a plump, rosy-cheeked Irish fella about nine years old, Joey. They are carving soap, animals out of soap.

Joey looks at Yitzchak's arm.

"Your name's Izzy, right? Why do people call you Numbers?"

"Because of my arm."

"Were you in prison?"

"Not really."

"My dad's a cop. I'm going to be a boxer. But I always get beat up."

"So why box?"

"My dad wants me to, that's why I'm here in this club."

"That looks good what you are making. A dog, right?"

"This is a lion."

"Could be an elephant or a lion."

"It's a lion. Last night I saw a lion."

"On TV or what?"

"Lions come in my room."

"You see them?"

"They talk to me."

"Like, what do they say?"

"They just talk to me. Sometimes they bite me. Once they bit my hands off. I couldn't box any more, till my hands grew back. Do lions come into your room?"

"No, but they come into my mother's room. They wake her up."

"She could shoot them. I'll make a pistol for her. I'll make a pistol for her and one for me."

"You don't need a pistol. Maybe just quit boxing."

"Why don't lions come in your room, Numbers?

"I don't know, Joey. Maybe I don't have the guts to let them in."

"You're afraid of lions?"

"I am, Joey. You got a lot of guts. More guts than I do. Here is your lion, Joey."

Joey picks up his jacket and starts to leave.

"I don't need it." Joey leaves.

Yitzchak takes the soap figure in his hands and mumbles,

" I do."

The lion won't turn back into soap. Yitzchak takes the subway home. When he gets home, Stacy has dinner waiting, but Yitzchak is still preoccupied with Joey's lion.

"Izzy, you don't like my cooking tonight?"

"I'm not too hungry. What time will you get back home?"

"Around 12. Might go for a drink with Ria. She's got some problems."

"I'll do some work tonight, if I'm not tired. I've got an idea."

"What kind of idea?"

"I don't know, an idea's got me."

"You all right?"

"Great. Let's not go to Antwerp this Chanukah. You've got the show anyway. I've had enough with Yom Kippur. I don't know… I mean I sang the Yom Kippur service in Antwerp sometimes. I did that for Mom and Pop and for myself, but I need a pause…Why don't we go to Ethiopia? Don't you miss Ethiopia?"

"Sure, I haven't been there for about three thousand years."

"Don't you miss the sphinxes?"

"Honey, the only sphinxes I know live in the Bronx. Harry and Joe Sphinx. The gay Sphinxes. I got to get a move on. I'll see you later."

"Have a good show!"

It is around midnight. Yitzchak is painting a very large canvas. He is trying to find a lion. He paints the basic form, paints eyes and the mouth and teeth and then paints them out and starts again. His face and hands are fighting to free something in the canvas. Suddenly his face appears where the lion's face was, his face snarling. Then he sees the lions that stand by the Ark in the synagogue in Antwerp and he sees the congregation in Antwerp. All these images swim in the canvas in front of him. He paints them out as fast as he can, but they keep coming back. He sees parts of bodies, a hand, a head, a leg. He tries to paint them out. The body parts seem to be trying to pull him into the painting. His face and clothes are covered with paint. Stacy comes into the loft.

"How's it coming?"

Yitzchak stares at her. He takes a bucket of red paint and throws it onto the canvas.

Later that night they are asleep. In his dreams Yitzchak is in a Roman amphitheater. Hungry lions prowl around looking for him. Suddenly he sees his father. He wakes up screaming, "Papa!!! Papa!!!"

Stacy wakes and puts her arms around Yitzchak.

"Let it go, baby. I'm here. I'm here."

Once the mind begins to bleed it is hard as hell to stop it. Yitzchak is sitting with a half empty bottle of vodka. He is staring at his tefillin which are on the table along with the prayer book and a yarmulke. He has been drinking since late morning. He is drunk. Stacy enters. She cautiously asks,

"What are you doing? Boy, that's a good idea. I've had one hell of a morning. Hugo telling me to leave the stage. I'm disturbing his fucking girlfriend. Maybe if she knew her role, she wouldn't be such a prima donna. Hey, you didn't leave me much. What are you doing, praying or drinking?"

"I'm dry-cleaning my brain."

"I thought Jews didn't drink."

"We play basketball. It's blacks that don't drink... What should I do with these?" Pointing to the tefillin.

"Izzy, Dad gave you those. You're drunk."

"I'm not drunk. I'm not anything. I'm not even here. There is a symbol of me here. The great white lover with the circumcised prick, the young painter, the good social worker, the devoted Jew, the Holocaust survivor. No, I'm not drunk. I'm not even drunk. I drank half a bottle of vodka and I'm not even drunk. You're pouring love into nothing. I am nothing. I don't even love you, Stacy. I'm trying to be honest. I'm a liar, trying to be honest."

"You know darling, sometimes you are a little tricky to live with. I think you need the other half of this bottle."

"I need a walk." He gets up with difficulty and stumbles out the door. Stacy sticks her head out the window and yells,

"And by the way, I love your white circumcised prick!"

Yitzchak is walking in a daze. The streets of Hell's Kitchen are filled with neighborhood life, people sitting on a stoop, just talking and watching life, kids playing stickball, teenagers in their late twenties, just standing and trading dreams and fears. A couple of kids recognize Yitzchak.

"Hey, Numbers, wanna play side car?"

Yitzchak is oblivious to the teaming street vitality. He sees a small church and wanders in. The inside of the church is cool, cool light, cool shadows. A simple pulpit. Near the pulpit is a simple cross with Christ nailed to it. Yitzchak sits in a wooden pew. He is alone. A priest enters. The priest is a ruddy Irish priest. He is in a hurry. He notices Yitzchak sitting in the pew, staring at the figure of Christ on the cross. A good priest knows when to ask, and when not to ask. He asks.

"Can I help you?

"You're a priest. Aren't you?"

"No, I just got dressed in a hurry this morning... Yes, I'm a priest."

"I work at the P.A.L."

"Are you looking for someone? "

"No, I just want to sit here. Is that all right?"

"Sure."

Yitzchak looks at the statue of the crucified Christ.

"I'm Jewish. I'm a Jew. I'm lost. I feel like Him. I thought they took Him down, took Him down to start again. But He's still nailed up there. We're all still nailed up there. Nails in our hands and feet and minds. I can't get down, Father. I think I'm down, I walk, even dance, but only in a dream. Every time I wake up, I see all of us nailed to a cross, nails in our hands. We send yearning looks to each other, but slaughter is so loud. We can hardly hear Christ's question, 'Lomo asavtoni?' – Why have You forsaken me?... Thank you for listening."

The priest looks at Yitzchak with concern. He speaks to him very gently.

"You're speaking from a very dark pool of blood, my son. A clever man could give you clever truths, but a wise man can only tell you the obvious. The obvious is love, only love. Love takes us down from the cross and gives us the power to live. You lost love. That is why you suffer. If you find love, you will live forever. If you don't, you will die. Like Christ was taken from us, someone was taken from you. Yes, we are still being crucified. The hammer is always pounding the spike and we deaden our ears with empty noise to keep from going crazy. But, my son, obviously love hasn't died. The evil forces have their work cut out for them, and they will have to pound forever because love will be forever— and, frankly, I would rather have a nail in my hand than a hammer. Go in peace, my son, and go in love."

Several weeks go by, weeks that strain the bond between Yitzchak and Stacy. Yitzchak continues to paint and to search in his painting for some element of real feeling, his real feeling. Stacy is patient, but patience can become sour, can turn into being simply being fed up. She watches him paint. His face is tense. His beard is a few days old. His voice is tight. He mumbles,

"Gefilltefish is coming over today."

"Who's Gefilltefish?"

"The art dealer... Fisher... Fishmann, whatever."

"Darling, that's fabulous. When's he coming?"

"I don't know, about three."

"Should we have some food or... I don't know... Darling. that's wonderful. Did he call or... "

"He called at the center. He got the slides and wants to see some stuff."

"Boy, you're pretty cool. Aren't you excited?"

"I'll see what he says. I hear he's a cold son of a bitch."

"Who cares? If he can get you a gallery. Are you hungry? I'm gonna fix lunch."

"I'm not hungry."

"You're losing weight. You want to be in the movies?"

"I'm not hungry, Stacy."

"Why are you calling me Stacy? Something wrong?"

"That's your name! Stacy. What do you want me to call you, Judy? I'm not hungry, Judy."

"Darling, what's wrong? You nervous about this Fishmann?

"I'm not fucking hungry, Stacy, Judy, whoever. I'm working and that's it."

"Should I be here when he comes?"

"This is your home. Why shouldn't you be here? He will look at some work and say what he has to say, and that's it."

"You keep saying that's it. What's it? What's up, Izzy?

"Nothing's up! I've got some work to do. I've got to do my work! I've got to find what I'm looking for… Look at this, Stacy, if you don't mind my calling you that. Look at this. This is bullshit."

"Are we bullshit too? We haven't made love in a month. Are we bullshit?"

"Not now Stacy!"

"When?!!!"

"OK… Look, there is some kind of a lie going on, yes, some kind of bullshit. We are not a man and a woman. We're a token, liberal, integrated couple. We're fucking Upper-West-Side liberals. Token goodie-goodies. We're so good I want to vomit. We don't scream and rage, we whine. We gather in support groups and whine. What's happened to our passion?… Do you think I'm really doing any good at the center? That's another lie."

"Of course you are. You're helping those kids."

"Bullshit. I'm putting band-aids on gashing wounds; I'm throwing band-aids at them and then congratulating myself. They don't need me; they need a different world. We're privileged, Stacy. We're shit luck privileged. Do you really want to know where I should be? I belong in a ditch filled with my people, my father, my mother, not here in Cutyville, not here in 'aren't-we-so-good-ville'!... Look at my work... Clever! Clever!... Boring!! This is all a lie. I'm a lie! We're a lie! Stacy, I've got to find my real self. If I didn't die, then I have to live, one or the other, nothing in the middle. If I can't believe myself then let the fucking Nazis have me. At least I'd be real. Stacy, I can't stand myself!!"

Stacy slowly and gently puts her arms around him. She whispers.

"What can I do my love, what can I do?"

Yitzchak screams, "Nothing!"

The doorbell rings.

"Nothing!" Doorbell rings again.

Stacy is startled.

"Oh my god! He's here."

"Let him in. Let the motherfucker in."

"Are you OK?"

"Yes, yes. I'm OK"

Stacy goes to the door, and lets Mr. Fishmann in. Mr. Fishmann is an ordinary-looking man, about 60, East-European face; only his eyes are not ordinary. They look like a radar-set, always moving, searching. His face is a question, and his eyes are looking for an answer. His voice is urgent.

"How do you do? I'm Fishmann."

Stacy regains her composure.

"Please come in, Mr. Fishmann."

"Am I disturbing?"

"No, no, come in. I'm Izzy. Thanks for coming. Do you want something to drink? Tea?"

"I don't have much time. What's your name? Izzy? Is that Isidore or Yitzchak?"

"My name is Yitzchak."

"Yitzchak ... Show me, Yitzchak. I don't have much time."

Yitzchak takes out several canvases. Fishmann glances at each, barely a second is spent on looking at each canvas. Fishmann notices the canvas that Yitzchak threw red paint on.

"What's that?"

"Oh, that's an accident."

"Let me see it."

Bringing the painting over, Yitzchak mumbles apologetically, "It's an accident."

Fishmann looks at the painting for a long time, his eyes resting on the painting's chaos. He speaks quietly.

"Was this painful?"

Yitzchak answers quietly,

"Yes."

Fishmann looks into Yitzchak's eyes.

"Can you stand it?"

"I don't know"

"If you can stand it, do more and I'll give you a show this spring. If you can't stand it, don't waste your time... or mine. I must go. Thank you for inviting me."

"Thank you for giving me your time."

As Fishmann is about to leave, he turns and looks at Yitzchak.

"Yitzchak... Your name is Yitzchak." He leaves.

Stacy is excited.

"Darling, I think he likes your work."

Yitzchak turns to look at his 'accident'.

"That's not important. That's not what just happened. He was here maybe five, maybe ten minutes. He saw everything. He didn't miss anything."

"But he wants to give you a show."

"He saw the stupid lie I'm living, and he saw my real life. He saw my arm and never mentioned it. Why? Because it's not important. Because, like my old teacher told me, all the rules, all the laws, all the misery that we must go through, is only to serve one purpose… to have the greatest love and respect for life. Life is the only thing that is important."

"When he left, he said your name is Yitzchak. Do you want to be called Yitzchak?"

"It's not important."

"Why did he say that?"

"It just means I am. I just am. We come into the world with stars in our crowns. Then violent people take the stars away. Fishmann just said I still have my stars. Maybe he means I have you. You can call me anything, darling. Just don't call me Judy."

###############

'Anti-Semitism' is an embarrassing word in our time. People don't want to hear it. Give the stage to other victims of racism they say, Black Americans for instance, or even better, Native Americans, or Palestinians, or… Of course, if this story were about equal time, the complaint would be justified. But it's not about equal time. It's about the life of a man named Sam, his wife Rachel and their son Yitzchak. It's about what happened one day in Antwerp as Sam was visiting a museum.

The museum has a special collection of Rubens paintings, huge rooms filled with the wealth of Rubens' genius. Sam is standing in awe of the famous painting 'Le coup de lance'. A guide is giving a tour, explaining the meaning of the paintings and, in a very matter of fact voice, giving the historical background of the works. He relates what year the 'Le coup de lance' was painted, and continues,

"The Jews wanted to hasten the death of the crucified men by breaking their legs. The Jewish law required that the men be dead and buried by sundown."

Sam walks over to the guide.

"What did you say?"

The guide professionally asks,

"Shall I speak up? Shall I speak louder? Are you with the group?"

Sam repeats,

"What did you say about the Jews breaking legs?"

The guide becomes annoyed.

"Please, this is a museum."

Sam hits the guide full in the face. Guards come and begin beating Sam. He is thrown out of the building.

Sam staggers down the street, his shirt torn, his nose bleeding. In a daze he wanders into a cathedral near the museum. He goes to the top of the cathedral and looks out onto the panorama that surrounds the city of Antwerp. The rooftops and the tiny humans are under him, but it is the light of Antwerp, the light in the sky that holds his eyes. He wonders what it would be like to live in that light. This is the light that dazed Rubens. Did Rubens also wonder what it is like to live on the other side of those blue grey clouds, to live in that golden light? A man is standing behind Sam. The man says quietly,

"Jump."

Sam is startled.

"What?"

The man continues quietly.

"The sky is special here. Excuse me." He indicates to Sam that Sam's nose is bleeding. Sam looks at the man confused. Sam wipes his nose. "Shit".

The man asks,

"Are you OK?"

"What do you want?"

The man offers his handkerchief.

Sam says,

      "I'm OK, I have a handkerchief."

The man smiles.

      "May I ask you something?"

      "What do you want to know?"

      "I saw what happened in the museum. I saw your arm."

      "So?"

      "You are a Jew, aren't you?"

      "I am an earthling."

The man asks seriously,

      "Please, it is important for me to know. "

      "Why is it important to you? Who are you?"

The man looks into Sam's eyes.

"No one. Do you think God lives on the other side of those clouds? Do you believe in God? If you're a Jew, you believe in God."

"I believe you're full of shit. What do you want?" Sam is trying to escape the man's stare.

"I want to know if you're a Jew."

"I'm a person."

"Then why were you so offended by the guide? He's only a person doing his job. He was only reciting the information on the pamphlet. That's his job. He was only doing his job."

"That was more or less Eichmann's argument."

The man presses on.

"Are you a Jew? Do you believe in God? Simple questions. What's your answer?"

Sam is losing his patience.

"I don't have to answer you."

The man remains cool.

"Yes, you do. For your sake, you do. Let's start with God. What's your answer?"

"God? I have no idea what you mean."

"Yes. God."

Sam begins to shout.

"God is a monster!! God is a sadistic joke! There. Are you satisfied?"

"No."

Sam is becoming hysterical.

"God is a sadistic powerful monster. God, or something... nature. Whatever name... we are here because of It. We... I... didn't choose to be here... anywhere... but we are here. No choice!!"

"Yes, choice."

"What are you telling me?"

"What are you telling yourself?"

Sam looks into the man's blank face.

"Did I hear you say jump? A few minutes ago… did you say jump?"

"Why not? People die. You know that. Excuse me, your family died. People die. Who are you? You think you won't die?"

Sam screams,

" Who are you?!!!"

The man answers calmly.

"I am only you. I am in your mind. Without you no one would be, me, God, no one. Your problem would be solved."

"What is this bullshit?"

The man moves toward the edge.

"I'm going now. Come with me."

"I have a covenant."

The man smirks.

"How touching. Did Rachel have a covenant? Did Yitzchak?"

75

Sam grabs the man by his shirt.

"Let them be!"

The man tries to push Sam away.

"Did God have a covenant with them? Did God fulfil His covenant by having them murdered? Come, Sam. You know too much. You can't wind your brain back to being ignorant. End this shit. Step into your friend Rubens' light."

Sam is desperate.

"I have a covenant."

"You said that."

"I have a covenant with THEM, with Yitzchak with Rachel!"

The man frees himself from Sam's grip.

"How romantic. Then continue your wonderful living, fuck whores, embrace your brilliant species, live your lie, tell yourself how meaningful

everything is, how hopeful. I'll wait. As they say, be well."
He turns to go.

"Wait, wait!" Sam yells, "You've started this, so let's continue. You're saying everything that exists is only in my mind, you, God, everything. I want my boy and I want my Rachel to stay alive, if only in my mind. For them to stay alive I must stay alive. I will stay alive for them! As long as there is a shred of me, then there will be a shred of them. Yes, there is a God! And God is not in my mind, I am in God's mind! There is nothing that I want from you. Not peace, not revenge, not justice —nothing. Wanting doesn't exist for me anymore. The me that you want to destroy doesn't exist. My footprints will always be behind me. I will never look back. I will never see my footprints again."
Sam walks away from the edge.

There is a tunnel in Antwerp. It goes under the Sheldt River. The tunnel is about 2.5 km long, about 8 metres wide and rounded at the top. The walls are made of swimming-pool green tiles. Sam's mind goes into this tunnel. He stands in the middle of the tunnel. He can't see the exit behind him nor the exit in front of him. Sam's mind slips into timelessness. He walks into the tunnel and listens to the sound of his mind's footsteps looking for a way out.

Sam saw himself as wounded. He tried to heal his wounds by writing. He tried to lift his mind into a higher place. He could stay among the low clouds or he could soar. Pain is accepted if it lifts. Somewhere in this Antwerp light sky, there must be the place where birds pause, where Sam's mind could pause. Sam filled his mind with words. His plays and stories were the droppings left to show that he had been. He forgot about the words as soon as they left his mind and produced new words, but it was all just mumbling, mumbling which had started those many years ago when he stumbled over the dead bodies as he walked

along the road away from Dachau.

###############

Sam went to his small room with a hot plate and wrote. He saw the few people he knew leave his life; the Friday visits to the woman who lit a candle stopped. The occasional glass of wine with friends became faded memories. Official letters from his bank and from tax-related institutions were left unopened in a pile of memories of another life. He began a search for another world where he could find peace. He wanted out of Egypt and so he left without taking time to bake bread. His mind went into the desert and his words were grains of sand, which stretched out to the sky. It was peaceful to watch the builders of Babel fade into the horizon. Sam found peace in isolation.

The problem with writing a play is that at some point it is finished, at least the first draft. Then what? What do you do with it? The idea of putting it in a suitcase filled with other plays and stories, a suitcase filled with paper, was too much like putting a newborn baby in a garbage can. The thing was there, alive, and it cried for the right to exist, if only for its brief few hours. Sam had this newborn thing in his hands and he loved it, not because it was good or bad, but just because it was. It needed to stumble and crawl and try to stand up and fall and then keep going until it could leave its creator so they both could get on with their lives. That was the problem with writing a play.

There was a small amateur theater in Antwerp, The Mobile Theater. Sam put his new play in a plastic bag and wandered over. It was raining. He quietly walked into a rehearsal and sat at the back and watched. Some young actors were seriously going about the business of enacting life, saying normal things as if they were thinking them on the spot, holding a script in their hand, glancing down at it inconspicuously, then saying things that people say. No one paid any attention to Sam. Somehow he just fitted in, a person wearing a raincoat sitting near the back of the small theater with a plastic bag in his hands. At a point when the rehearsal seemed to dissolve, Sam stood up and walked over to a man who appeared to be the director. The man had short white hair, wore glasses, had a short nose and smoked cigarettes while he worked.

Sam cleared his throat. He hadn't spoken to anyone in several months, other than muttering 'excuse me' when he accidentally bumped into someone on the street.

"Excuse me. I, well I wrote this play and was wondering whom I might speak to about getting a reading. My name is Sam Levine."

The man looked at Sam over his glasses.

" You're a playwright?"

"Well, yes. I've written a few plays."

"We're an amateur group."

"I was wondering how I might go about getting a reading."

"We sometimes do original works. Is that your play?" The man nodded to the plastic bag.

"Yes."

"Ever do any acting?"

"Not if I can help it."

The man smiled.

"My name's Kehoe, Ted Kehoe."

They shook hands.

"What kind of play?"

"That's why I want a reading. It might be a comedy. Might not. It started out as a comedy, but the stars moved. By the time you finish a play the stars aren't in the same place as they were when you started. We look up at them, get their position, but by the time their light has reached us, the stars have moved on, so you never know what you've ended up with. That's why I need a reading."

"How many characters?"

"Two. A man and a woman."

"Mind if I take a look at it? You have another copy?"

"I have several copies."

Sam gave Kehoe the plastic bag.

"I'll take a look at it. Give me a few days."

"I'll come by next week,"

Sam turned to leave the theater. Kehoe watched him walk away. He called,

"Sam, what do you call your play? Has it got a name?"

Sam turned.

"The Wine Bottles."

The reading was interesting. There was no point in trying to conclude anything. The two actors read the lines and Sam and Kehoe listened, both hearing the play for the first time, both wondering if and when things would make sense. When the last lines were read, a kind of blue energy filled the theater like when someone dies and peace fills the room. Struggle is over. Everything that had been so important vanishes, and where the stars are doesn't matter anymore. That meant that the play was good.

Sam left the theater wondering why he had written the play, why he had written any play. What was the point? He always came back to the same place, the blank page. Was it possible to write a play that would make a permanent change in mankind, like a mutation and even a mutation was only a false prophet? 'Now things will be different,' says the new molecule, but when the celebration is over and the fittest have survived, the fittest are stuck with the same question. Where are the stars now? The stars weren't anywhere. They just were, entirely unto themselves. Putting them somewhere wasn't necessary. That made the human condition a phenomenon outside the possibility of conclusion, just go on forever, which meant it would.

Kehoe agreed to put the play on and rehearsal began.

Sam's play was set on a strip of sand about twenty meters wide, poured onto the stage, and a translucent screen was behind the strip of sand. The sand was smooth. A film of ocean waves was projected onto the translucent screen from behind. It was night. One heard the sound of waves gently lapping onto the beach. Oily moonlight filled the stage. A bearded man walked onto the beach. He left footprints in the smooth sand. He stopped and looked out into the sea, his back to the audience. The wanderer wore a sea cap. His long greying hair touched his slightly bent back. He wore an old threadbare coat and carried a worn leather suitcase. A woman from the audience came up on the stage. She had long sandy blond hair with streaks of white. A large fan blew a currant of air across the stage and her hair moved as if blown by an ocean breeze. She wore a long, pale, loose-fitting dress. The wind held the soft fabric close to her body. Her voice was warm and deep.

"Where are you going?"

The wanderer turned to face her. His grizzly grey beard softened his leathery face. His eyes were blue grey like the ocean waves. His voice was grizzly like his beard.

"I didn't know that anyone was here. I didn't see you."

"I was over there." (nodding toward the audience) "Where are you headed?"

"Here. I'm headed here."

"Where are you from?"

"I think I'm from here. I've been away, different places. I'm back now."

"Will you stay?"

"I don't know. There are things to see. Do you always stay here?"

"Always."

"I'll stay a while for sure. I'm sick of seeing things. Sometimes I wish I were blind."

"Blind people see what you're sick of seeing."

"Is there anybody else here?"

"Not now."

"I'll just sit here. It sure feels good to sit here."

"You'll probably be moving. You'll get itchy and want to move on."

"Think so? Maybe. You're always here? You make your own bread? Make your own wine?"

"Bread, I make my own bread."

"I always wanted to make my own wine. If you stay in one place, you can do that. I always wanted to do that, part of me; the other part of me wants to drink wine from somewhere else, different countries. I wonder what happens when I can't move any more, when slowly the distances become shorter and shorter, till I wind up in just one place. You're in just one place. How is that? Just being here?"

"I'm everywhere. Being here is like being anywhere else. Look at all that water. It moves within itself. It stays in one place and moves. It might be like that for you when you don't travel any more. You'll be like the sea."

"Anyway when I stop it will only be for a rest. Then I'll pack my bag and head off into space. Plenty of room there."

"What did you see that made you sick?"

"It's like being surrounded by beggars, like in India, thousands of beggars, some wear suits or uniforms or rags but it all amounts to the same thing. They stretch out their hands with their palms up and their thumbs in a funny yearning position. Their faces smile in pain. It's a matter of life or death to them. Pleading for money, for votes, for love. Presidents and prostitutes with the same face. Then they kill each other. Smart or dumb, doesn't make any difference when your dead. Part of me wants to look around and part of me just wants to run away. When I stop, the beggars suffocate me. Besides, I just like to look around."

"Are you looking for someone?"

"I don't want to talk about that."

"Why not?"

"They don't exist. The people I'm looking for don't exist."

"They exist."

"They exist until they evaporate."

"Everybody exists until we evaporate. This whole universe will evaporate."

"You're a funny woman."

"You're a funny man."

Sam watched the rehearsal and lived in it. It was better than living outside it. Sam wrote his play like God wrote His play, so He could exist until He evaporated.

The lights began to come up slowly on the strip of sand. The wanderer and the woman sat watching the morning sky. The wanderer found it interesting that the black night didn't end and suddenly become bright morning, but rather first there was the lightest of blue in the sky, hardly perceptible. Then, with incredible patience, light slowly filled the space and morning gently dominated. The wanderer thought of an old Arabic saying. His gravelly voice spoke over the sound of the lapping waves.

"Haste belongs to the Devil and patience belongs to God."

"Who are you looking for?"

"You mean the Devil or God?"

"You said you were looking for someone who doesn't exist."

"I'm looking for the continuation of myself."

"What if you don't continue? What if you just are, forever?"

The wanderer smiled.

"It would certainly take the heat off."

Waves lapped against the shore. The wanderer continued,

"I don't think the place I'm looking for exists either. We live in boxes, but the boxes we live in are not our homes. Why do we collect living-places, time-places?"

"We don't collect them. They collect us."

"I guess I'm just trying to avoid the collection man."

"You mean you're afraid."

"Very afraid."

"I think it's a question of patterns. After a while we all get into some sort of pattern. If the pattern becomes a box, then we've been collected."

"Seeing people in a box makes me sick. Seeing myself in a box terrifies me."

"Then your box is fear."

"I guess I have to live with that."

"Are you more God or the Devil?"

"I think I'm more an impatient God, which might be what the Devil is. It's like hate and love. I hate not loving."

"What happened to the people you're looking for?"

"I don't want to talk about it. I leave notes for them in bottles, in wine bottles. I put the bottles in the sea and the bottles float away. One day the people I'm looking for will wake up surrounded by thousands of wine bottles, all from me."

"What happened to them?"

"They were gathered."

"Like crops?"

"Their day ended."

"They're out there in the sea? Waiting for your bottles?"

"Maybe they're putting notes for me in bottles and I'll find them on the shore."

"Maybe. Let's take a walk."

The wanderer and the woman walk off the stage, leaving footprints in the smooth sand.

Sam watched and listened to his play leave his mind and become peopled. He didn't know the people. He had written about them, but as they insisted on being out of his life and into their own, he didn't know what they would do anymore. They had their lives, his words but their lives. He wanted to go somewhere else, be a different person, thinner, fatter, different. He wanted to rewrite his life, climb out of the boxes he had been living in. He didn't stay for the premiere. Everything which had been so important became ghosts that he needed to run from. Goodbye everything. Sam never saw the last rehearsals; never saw the audience part of the cycle of playwriting. Why had everything been so important? He wanted so much to write himself as someone else, to show up in a new place like a sailor who would spend some time in a port, not far from the land's fringe, just in case he wanted to go back to sea. He wanted to go to a place where it would always be morning, early morning, before people arrived. He wanted to live in the time of potential, before any event occurred. Sam went to his room with the hot plate and shut the door.

His play opened. The audience was mostly friends. The critic from the press noticed the absence of the playwright. Why would a playwright not be at his own premiere? Intriguing. Who was this Sam Levine? The critics were good. Lyric, poetic, thought-provoking, but who was its author? Where was its author? Kehoe had no address for him, no phone number.

Kehoe explained to the young critic.

"He just showed up one day and toward the end of the rehearsal period he just didn't show up any more, just disappeared. Maybe he's sick. I hope not. I don't think so, but maybe he's sick. I don't know how to reach him. Strange guy, nice, quiet."

The young critic was curious. She was very curious. There was a story here. The author was a sensitive person, obviously, sensitive and, at least in his mind, restless. Did he just get boxed in like the character in his play and take off? She decided to find him. Sam Levine. Had he written anything else? She looked him up and found out that he had written a successful play a few years ago called Real Estate. He was from Belgium, had lost his family in the war. All this was on file. He must be living somewhere here in Belgium, maybe here in Antwerp. Real Estate was premiered in Tel Aviv. Maybe this Mr. Levine was Jewish. Maybe the Jewish community in Antwerp could help her.

Annika Nielson was Swedish and stubborn. She had a clean blond beauty. She looked about as Jewish as Muhammad Ali. Wandering around in the diamond district in Antwerp, she felt very much in the minority. Her first stop was a restaurant called 'Lama Lo'. 'Lama lo' was Hebrew for "why not". A good place to begin. All she got from her first efforts were some stares and a very good, somewhat expensive, Middle Eastern meal. She went to a synagogue, again no information, to small bookstores, which also sold religious articles, no success. Some people she asked rudely avoided her, others wanted to help her. They seemed to understand her need to locate someone. After several weeks she got nowhere. There were hundreds of Levines in the neighborhood; a few would-be playwrights, but no Sam Levine, author of Real Estate.

Maybe Mr. Levine wasn't Jewish, at least in any active sense of the word. Even a recluse had to eat. Maybe he lived near the theater. Kehoe said he showed up one day at the theater with his play in a plastic bag. A grocery bag? She asked Kehoe.

"What kind of bag?"

"It was a plastic bag, an Aldi bag."

"Is there an Aldi around here?"

"There are several."

"Do you think he lives around here?"

"Maybe. I don't think he had much money. He wore an old raincoat, old cream-colored raincoat, rarely took it off."

Annika located the Aldi stores in the vicinity of the theater. There were three. She spent the next few weeks cruising Aldis. She worked during the day, so her private quest to find Sam Levine took place after work. A man in a raincoat, around fifty-five, medium height, greying hair, blue eyes, that's how Kehoe had described him. It was cold. It rained almost every day. Priorities began to shift. "Why in hell am I doing this? Is it the father shit again?" she wondered.

Annika's father had been a wanderer. But it was boring to always have women looking for their fathers and men looking for their mothers. So she found this Sam Levine, so what. She'd write an article about some old codger who lived outside the norm, another story about some latter-day Bohemian, and people would read her article while waiting for a bus, or during the reserved period in the morning between finishing coffee and going to work. In either case the paper would end up in the wastebasket.

Besides, she had caught a cold. She stopped off at a drugstore to pick up some cold medicine. The drugstore was crowded. It was the sick season. She stood in line to be served. She felt stupid getting sick trying to find some nut who didn't come to his own play's premiere. The line wasn't moving fast enough. The man in front of her seemed lost in a dream. Then she noticed he was wearing a cream-colored, wrinkled raincoat. She noticed he didn't wear a hat and that his hair was unkempt and greying. An electric spark went through her. She quietly spoke to him.

"Excuse me." The man turned around. He had grey blue eyes. "Excuse me. Are you Sam Levine?" The man had to clear his voice several times before he spoke.

"Yes."

"I'm Annika Nielson. I saw your play, The Wine Bottles."

Sam looked at her gently, waiting to hear what she would

say next.

She continued,

"It's a beautiful play. You wrote a play

called Real Estate."

"Yes."

"I've been looking for you."

"Why?"

"I don't know. Why weren't you at the

play's opening?"

"I was at the play's opening. It opened

when I started to write it."

"I mean at the theater opening, the opening

at the Mobile theater."

"Why?"

"To celebrate."

"Celebrate?"

"Celebrate the new life, the play's new life."

"Do you think the play missed me? "

"If I were a play, I'd want my author to be there when I was born."

"Was your author not there when you were born?"

"He went to sea, like your wanderer."

"Do you have a cold?"

"Yes."

"It's the season for colds."

"I'd like to write an article about you for my paper. Would you mind?"

"You have a paper?"

"I work for the Antwerp News. I'm just getting started. Reporter, I'm a reporter. I'm Annika."

They both bought cold medicine and left the drugstore.

The rain had stopped, but it was cold. Annika invited Sam to have a coffee. Sam let himself be seduced, not by this young woman, but by human warmth. Annika took over. Sam watched himself follow. They went to a coffee shop and Sam, who normally drank tea with lemon on such a night, allowed Annika to order two coffees. He looked at her. He hadn't looked at anyone who lived outside his inner world in a long time. He watched her face, her blue eyes. She believed in her actions. Only occasionally did she stop as if to question her self-confidence, as if to look to see if he was still there. She asked,

"Do you care?"

"You mean the article?"

"No, I mean what do you care about. Do you care about anything? What do you care about?"

"Is this an interview?"

"No. You didn't care to come to the opening of Wine Bottles."

"I care about everything. I care about not being seduced into believing in something I don't believe in."

"What don't you believe in?"

"Trust."

"You don't trust anything?"

"I like early mornings. Early morning is free from weight, like a beach you're the first to step onto. Pink flamingos fluttering up, trying to get away from you, though you mean them no harm. You walk onto the sand, swapping weightless floating where you had little control of your movements, for being weighted and having a lot of control of where you want to go, except you don't want to go anywhere. You just want to stand up. You're strapped to the planet, but only the planet... I haven't talked with anyone in a while. Excuse me, I'm getting a little windy."

"Do you trust anything else, anything other than early morning?"

"I like tea with lemon, a little sugar."

"What about the article?"

"I don't think I'm entertaining enough as a person in a room. People like my plays but just to write about a person who drinks tea and doesn't care to celebrate would be boring. You would lose your job."

"Does that mean I can write the article?"

"Don't tell anyone where they can find me. Don't say where I am."

"I'll say I'm writing from another city, Ghent."

"We can meet here, in this restaurant. Do you want some chicken soup?"

"Yes. The paper will treat us to chicken soup."

"It's late. Is someone waiting for you?"

"I have a daughter, six, she's with her father tonight."

"You're divorced?"

"We were never married."

A waiter came by and they ordered chicken soup.

"How long were you not married?"

"About seven years."

"Writers are too curious. We ask too many questions."

"Fair is fair."

"Do you love him?"

"No. I used to. I had a caesarean. The scar was swollen for a long time. I was fat after the birth. He made fun of me. He forced me one night. It hurt a lot. I didn't love him after that."

"But you stayed with him."

"For the child."

"For the child?"

"He could also be very nice. He had his character. Everybody has faults."

"You could have left him."

"I'm used to people like him. My parents were always fighting. They separated when I was young, we were young. I have a brother. He is dark, I mean his hair. Black. My brother and my husband, ex-husband, hate each other. My ex once threw a glass of wine at me and my brother hit him in the nose. I'm used to all that. He helps me with the child. He can be very nice."

"Like your father?"

"My father was busy with his women and the sea. My brother and I weren't so important, so we made ourselves important. We got slapped for it but we became important for a while. Sometimes being slapped is a secret form of being loved."

"I never hit my son."

"You have a son?"

"I lost him. I never hit him."

"I'm used to it."

"Do you get used to it?"

"Sometimes he's nice."

"Isn't that the worst thing that can happen, getting used to it?"

Annika and Sam agreed to meet the next evening. She would bring her tape recorder.

Sam got to the restaurant at eight o'clock. Annika was sitting at a table in the back of the restaurant. Sam didn't see her at first when he came in. He thought she might have changed her mind. When he finally spotted her, she looked like a movie star. She was wearing sunglasses. They were black and looked glamorous against her blond hair. He walked to the table and sat down. She extended her hand and a smile. Sam liked the sunglasses-look, but he wanted to see her eyes. She ordered coffee and a cup of tomato soup. Sam ordered chicken soup and tea with lemon. Annika took out her small tape recorder and put it on the table between them. While they ate, Annika wore the sunglasses. When they finished eating, she took the sunglasses off and turned on the tape recorder. Her face was swollen. She had a black eye.

She explained,

"We had a scene last night when I went to pick up my child. He's jealous. Wanted to know why I was late in picking her up."

"My God. Did you call the police?"

"It wasn't necessary. He calmed down."

"Why do you stay with him?"

"We're supposed to be talking about YOUR life,"

"Why do you stay with him?"

"He can be nice."

"Hitler was nice to his dogs."

"Why is it important to you?"

"I hate tyrants."

"I appreciate your concern, but I want to talk about you, your life."

"We ARE talking about my life."

"You said you lost your son."

"A tyrant killed him."

"Your wife?"

"Also."

"I'm sorry. Maybe you don't want to talk about it. We don't have to."

"That's the point. We DO have to talk about it. If you want to talk about me, my life, then we have to talk about what I will do with the rest of it. You are just as much a victim as my family was. You are a victim of yourself. You have the choice they didn't have. You can leave. They couldn't. If you don't leave, you will become one of them. You will become the tyrant. I don't co-operate with tyrants. I think our interview is over."

"Wait, Mr. Levine. Please. It's not so simple. Things are not always black or white."

"When you are free from this person, we can continue, until then, forget that you found me."

"If I leave him, he will turn my child against me."

"If you don't leave, YOU will turn your child against you. You will teach your child resignation, even cruelty. You'll teach your child to take the side of evil, to not have any belief in human values, only in the power of force. Your friend, or whatever he is, is sick and so are you. But you can change the course of your child's future and your own future. That's the meaning of my life, the life you want to write about, to change the direction people are going in."

"You won't do that by being a recluse. If you want to make judgments about my life, then I can make judgments about yours. You can write. You can reach people. Why do you hide yourself? Isn't that giving in to some fear just like my being afraid?"

"I haven't stopped writing."

"Your Wine Bottles doesn't belong to amateur theater. It should have the same chance as Real Estate. It belongs on the stage where people can see it."

"I write the plays. What happens after that is not in my hands."

"Then put it in your hands. Maybe I can help you."

"You? You can't even help yourself. You willingly live with a fascist and you want to help me."

"I don't live with him."

"You don't stop him from abusing you. You could call the police. You could put a restraining order against him. Do you enjoy it?"

"Excuse me?"

"Do you enjoy being hit and abused? Why didn't you report him to the police?"

"I have reported him. He doesn't do it so often now. I need him to help me with our child. I can't work and take care of her without help."

"Then get help from someone who isn't a fascist. Other mothers do, single mothers."

"I don't want her to grow up without her father. I did and I can tell you, it's not nice."

"You call a man who hits his wife a father? Does he hit the child?"

"Of course not."

"It's a question of time, Annika. It's a question of time. When she is older and has her own mind, she'll learn what you learned, that attention comes in the form of abuse. He loves her 'enough to hit her'. 'It hurts him more than it hurts her', bullshit! 'It's for her own good.' She'll expect abuse from her partner just like you do. She'll even do things to make him abuse her, just like you do."

"Just like I do?!"

"You said he's jealous. You knew he would be angry if you came late to pick her up"

"Excuse me. I have a right to do my work. Sometimes I work late."

"I know that but you don't have his permission to be late."

"I don't NEED his permission."

"Tell HIM that. Tell him and he will knock the hell out you, and you KNOW it. And you WANT it. Otherwise you would tell him to go to hell. Take your child and tell him to drop dead. Believe me, I know women who wouldn't stand for the way you are treated for one second. Annika, you want to be abused. You have a choice millions of women who are rotting under the ground didn't have. You CHOOSE to stay with a monster who is sometimes nice. You insult the dignity of women who had no choice. You disgust me. I'll take care of my own future. Your point is made about my being a recluse. I can't stand being a part of this society I live in. It's made its mark on me. I'm frightened. I admit it. But I won't have any part in the life you lead. I won't converse with a WILLING victim! It insults people I love."

"Sam, please."

"Get rid of him or get lost."

"I only want to help you."

"The Nazis told the people they put in concentration camps that they were doing it for their own good, to protect them. That's what they told them. Then they slaughtered them. You are either with them or against them, black or white. Dead people aren't in a gray zone. Your help is a killing help."

"Sam, you're paranoid."

"Thank GOD! Being healthy on your terms is horrible. I'm leaving, Annika. I know why I live like I do. It's because of people like you, normal people who accept being the victims of dictators, politicians, people who learned as a child to get used to it, people who don't have the courage or the will to break the chain of abuse." Sam got up and went back to his room with the hot plate. He never saw Annika again.

###############

The shapes of the Hebrew letters, the very black shapes, the curves and black ink drops had a life apart from their literal meaning. They were poems of form crying to be understood. 'We are not words. We are shapes. Our meaning is mysterious and noble, not contained in language, but in how we occupy space.' Aleph, Bet, the letters sang in time. They sang in Yitzchak's throat. He didn't understand their meaning, but when he sang them, time was still and terrifying. He woke Stacy up in the middle of the night to tell her that the Hebrew letters were terrifying and she understood and went back to sleep and the next morning she forgot about being wakened up and was surprised to find Yitzchak naked, painting Hebrew letters.

"What in the world are you doing?"

"I don't know, but aren't they magnificent?"

Stacy stood naked, next to Yitzchak. She looked at the black letters floating on the canvas.

"They are magnificent. Do you want some coffee?"

"Later."

They went back to bed.

Yitzchak made many paintings of Hebrew letters and he placed the paintings against the walls and some were hung on the walls. The paintings were very black and very white, like letters on a page in a prayer book or on the Torah scroll. One afternoon he came home from work and began to fix lunch. He was alone. Stacy was rehearsing. It was a fall afternoon. The sun was bright and light poured into his studio. He took a smoked fish out of the refrigerator and cut the fish across the middle. His hands were getting oily from the fish and Yitzchak began to smell the smoked fishy smell that some people liked and some people didn't. He had the knife in his hand as he glanced at the painting of the Hebrew letters. A dark red color appeared to be dripping from the top of one of the letters; the color was seeping out of the letter. The color began to run down the painting.. Yitzchak stood at the kitchen table with the knife in his hand and watched the red color drip down the painting. He wasn't frightened by what he saw. He continued to cut the fish into small slices and then he poured himself a small glass of vodka and then cut some black bread with the fishy knife. The painting continued to bleed the red color. Yitzchak walked over to the painting with the small glass of vodka in one hand and the knife in the other. He looked closely at the moving color. Soon the whole letter was dripping red paint. The color was running into the white area around the letter. Yitzchak sipped the vodka slowly. He finished the glass and let it fall to the floor. He pushed the point of the knife into the wrist of his free arm, the arm with the number on it. His arm began to bleed. Yitzchak watched the red blood come out of his arm. At first the blood came out slowly. Yitzchak pushed the point of the knife deeper into his arm and the blood came out faster. Soon it was pulsing out of his arm to the rhythm of his heartbeat. He placed the bloody side of his arm on the painting.

When Stacy came home, she found Yitzchak lying unconscious in a pool of blood at the foot of the painting. The painting was covered with Yitzchak's blood.

Suicide is not well looked upon in the Jewish religion, but Yitzchak explained to Stacy that he hadn't attempted suicide. He had simply finished the painting. Yitzchak lay in the hospital bed with his wrist taped up, trying to understand what he had done.

"Blood is life and the letter was dead without my blood. I wanted to give it life, all the dead letters in my books must be brought back to life, otherwise they'll just lie there in the books like corpses in a ditch, millions of corpses."

"You can't bring the corpses back to life, darling."

"Stacy, there's something wrong with me. I saw the letters bleed. They started to bleed. I really think I'm going crazy or something. When I did those paintings that Fishmann liked, it was the same thing. The paintings were alive. Bodies, bloody bodies were alive in the painting. I hallucinate or something. I think I... I don't know. I think I'm crazy."

"I'm sure it's connected to your past, when you were a boy, in that horrible camp with your dad. It's understandable that that horrible time in your life would leave its marks. You told me that you might, I think you said, thaw. Things, memories, emotions would start to come back to you."

"I remember that night. We were talking about my mother in Antwerp, how she couldn't sleep because old memories were keeping her awake at night. You said that if that happened to me that I should just let it go. You said 'Let it go baby, I'm here.'

Stacy sat on the bed and put her arms around Yitzchak.

"Let it go baby. I'm here."

The wrist healed. There was a scar, but it healed. Yitzchak's left arm was becoming a strange work of art. He received psychiatric treatment at the hospital, a brief conference with a therapist and later he was an outpatient, visiting the therapist every week for a few months. The therapist helped Yitzchak to understand that the Hebrew letters symbolized the bodies in the ditch he was thrown into, he and his father.

"Do you remember your father?"

"No. Not really. I have a stepfather in Antwerp. I can't remember my real father. I was young."

"Can you remember what he looked like?"

"No. I probably look like him."

"Do you think he survived?"

"Everybody was killed, shot. They all died."

"You didn't die."

"Sometimes I wish I had."

"Do you feel guilty that you didn't die?"

"Why should I feel guilty? I didn't do anything. I was just a kid. I didn't do anything."

Yitzchak's face twisted. He screamed,

"I didn't do anything! I was just a kid! A boy! I didn't do anything!" Tears and anguish flooded into his face. "I was just a little kid."

Yitzchak and the therapist sat in the therapist's office until Yitzchak slowly regained his composure.

"If your paintings start to move again, call me. Night or day, call me. Is it a deal?"

"Do you think he is alive?"

"I'll answer you in a very unprofessional way. Only God knows if your father is alive. Only God knows."

Yitzchak left the therapist's office. It was night. He started to walk. His mind fell into a pit. He felt he was losing his grip. He felt his arms around his father's neck and his father's arms around him and then his father's arms were gone and he was flung into space. He felt himself fall into frozen white stillness. The pain was sudden. It was being alone forever.

A year passed. Yitzchak and Stacy lived on eggshells. The episode with the Hebrew letters threw caution into their lives together. Yitzchak let his paintbrushes rest. He put his collection of paintings in a corner and concentrated on his work at the center. Stacy went about her career. She was rehearsing a play called Real Estate. She played the role of

a woman who was forced to sexually accommodate

German soldiers in order to remain alive. In the end she was

murdered along with millions of other victims. The play

had gained some recognition since its premiere in Israel

some years before. No one knew much about the play's

author, only that he had written a few plays and then

disappeared. Yitzchak and Stacy found it interesting that

the author's name was Levine. Maybe he was related.

Yitzchak saw a few performances, but found the story to be

melodramatic, exaggerated. He and Stacy had many

arguments about the play. Yitzchak felt that the woman was

immoral.

He argued,

"I just don't see how she can be considered

some kind of hero. She had a husband. OK, she had to save

her life, or at least try, but what kind of life was she saving?

She betrayed her husband, her own dignity, her people, and

she was killed anyway. So what kind of message is that? We should just let ourselves be used and give up our dignity so we can have a few more years of being shit all over."

"Maybe she thought the nightmare would come to an end and she would take up her life again. "

"How could she take up her life again? After something like that, being forced to fuck her own murderers. What life was left to take up?"

"She wouldn't know unless she was alive to find out. Sometimes you can turn something horrible into something good."

"Stacy, you can't turn her life into something good. It's times like this that I feel that you're a real Pollyanna American. Excuse me, but I'm sorry. Her life was over when she was arrested, when she was put into that camp, whichever one it was. That's the reality. I don't know. Maybe I would have done the same thing she did, try to save my life, but I wouldn't think of myself as some kind of a hero."

"You took something horrible and turned into something good, into your work with your kids, into your painting."

"Right, and look where it got me. I almost killed myself. Those goddamned Hebrew letters. I'm afraid to even go near my tefillin, my prayer book. That's the good that came out of my horrible experience."

"Are you blaming God for your fate?"

"Who else?"

"What about the PEOPLE who put some sick mentally crippled psychopath in a position of power? This God that you want to blame, this God that has so much power over our lives, who thought this God up? Sounds to me like you have created some holy critter who will relieve you of any responsibility for your own life. How many blades of grass know about this God? How many birds?

How many breezes? How many rose buds know about this phenomenon you call God? Of course birds and breezes aren't as important as humans. They're not on the stock exchange. They don't speak any of our languages. They're below the human level on the 'hit the gong of importance' game. You, my love, are at least, a little responsible for your fate."

"Right. It is my fault that I was in a fucking concentration camp."

"It is your responsibility to hope."

"That's it, Pollyanna? That's what your play wants to tell us? Hope against hope. I love you, Stacy, but let's get one thing clear. You don't know, thank God, you don't know what the fuck you're talking about."

"The author of the play doesn't seem to think so. This Levine guy doesn't seem to have given up hope. He thinks he can reach an audience, make them aware, change the world."

"Excuse me, but what the hell does he know? Was he THERE? Does he have a shimmer of an idea what it must have been like? He's probably some Jew who has read a lot about the camps. Maybe someone in his family was murdered. HOPE? Kiss my ass! Hope is for people who never had a reason to NOT hope."

"Hope is the only option we have. If there's no hope, we can pack our bags and go the way of the dinosaur."

"I love you, Stacy. Maybe that's what you mean by hope. If that's what you mean, then let's hope we eat breakfast. I'm hungry."

Yitzchak longed for Antwerp. He longed to wander the streets, the ghetto. He hadn't seen his step-parents in several years. Stacy was between shows and he was on sick leave. Off they went.

After the plane and the train, they arrived in the station in Antwerp. Yitzchak's parents met them and they took a short cab ride to their home in the ghetto. It was home and Jewish food and streets filled with Chassidic costumes. It was the man who sold fish and looked like a fish. It was calm Mr. Morivitz who owned the kosher meat store and extended his elbow in greeting, his elbow and a glass of tea with hard sugar on the side. It was the synagogue where Yitzchak had spent his teenage years learning the Hebrew letters. The posters of the Jewish alphabet still hung on the old classroom walls. It was the smell of time that lived in old buildings. And it was the light in the Antwerp sky, the clean blue hidden behind the smoky grey with touches of rich gold tinges. It was the old stores that sold herring where the fat round women, who wore wigs and hadn't moved from their sitting positions for years, asked if you wanted the salty Russian herring with onions. It was signs written in Belgian and Yiddish. It was the stores that sold gold and diamonds and the dark narrow leaning stores which contained towers of books written in Hebrew. It was Antwerp.

Rain fell from the sky. It fell down and slightly sideways. Yitzchak and his step-father were sitting in the living-room, watching the rain through the window.

"I've seen scars like that, son."

"Papa, I'm losing my mind. I'm surrounded by love and still I feel myself crying, 'Why am I alone? Why? Why?' My mind won't help me. You've nourished my mind, but my mind won't help me, won't stop the pain. Why Papa? Why?"

"If the mind could stop the pain of lost love, then it wasn't love. We human beings, we weep. Even the heavens weep. It's our destiny. Like joy is our destiny, weeping is our destiny. It's in our prayers, the weeping. Our souls are filled with joy and with power, but also with pain. It's our destiny."

"I miss him so much, Papa. I miss him so much. I don't even know him. But he's alive in me. I love you and Mom, but God in heaven, I miss him."

"I don't know him either, son. But I miss him too. But weeping is better than cutting."

Yitzchak and Stacy attended the Shabbos prayers. Stacy sat upstairs, among the women. She wore a small handkerchief on her head. Yitzchak sat downstairs among the men. Yitzchak's stepfather sang the service.

Yitzchak had gotten up early, put on his tefillin, put on a suit, even a tie. Stacy rarely saw Yitzchak wear a suit, much less a tie. She wore a simple dark suit and after breakfast they all went to the synagogue with a strange 'dressed up in the morning' feeling and jet lag. Stacy watched the service from over a balcony, upstairs. She was filled with curiosity and respect, mixed with occasional boredom. The droning of the prayers, the ancient sound of ritual, the bearded men dressed in black silk robes and large fur hats, the women wearing 'proper attire' which avoided sexual signals, the children scampering freely among the formality, the beautiful sound of her father-in-law's tenor voice surrendering to Jewish history all made Stacy feel apart from, but welcome, in this private world of Yitzchak's early life. She watched him from the balcony. It was strange to watch someone you love from so far above. She could see his face as he stood holding the prayer book, the creamy white prayer shawl with the fringes dangling from its corners over his shoulders. He looked comfortable, peacefully bobbing back and forth singing the prayers. She thought of her little Baptist church and how they swayed from side to side when they sang instead of forward and backward. Maybe she would take Yitzchak home to her little Baptist church some day.

The prayers gave Yitzchak comfort in some way. He sang and mumbled in Hebrew. The words meant something but Yitzchak didn't really think about the meaning. It was like swimming in warm water, water that sang. He moved with the waves of sound and the waves of energy coming out of the people next to him. His voice gained strength. He didn't know why or care. The old feeling, the feeling of wholeness filled him. He was becoming one with Something.

When the last prayer was sung by the congregation and the men took off their prayer shawls and casually folded them and returned them to velvet bags, Yitzchak went over to his father and embraced him.

"Gut Shabbos, Papa."

His eyes were filled with love.

"Papa. Why do people hurt each other? Why do people not love each other?"

His stepfather held his son's head in his soft hand.

"Gut Shabbos, Yitzchak. When will we hear your voice again on this bima?"

"I think I've forgotten how everything goes."

"I'll help you remember.

###############

The beach is rough. The sea grass clings to the sand. It's a windy day, not a day for the timid or the melancholy, more like a casino day, a gambling day. Maybe the clouds will turn into a tornado. Maybe the sea will quit galloping and break into a thundering run, not meant to harm anyone but if someone is in the way, then 'this is our part of town baby'. You might get playfully destroyed or let's say you might not be in your element. And that is where Sam is. He has built a shelter in a dip in the dunes. The structure is mainly made of driftwood and old blankets and an abandoned piece of plastic held down with large rocks and magic. There is a small fire where he has boiled water for tea. The camp is strangely quiet in terms of wind, out of the strong currents, quiet and just right. Suddenly a naked Sam springs out of the top of a dune and runs like a wild horse into the playful sea. He has grown older and somewhat ripe, beard and hair uncombed, thinner and older muscles that would constitute the cheaper meat cuts in a butcher shop, both wild and peaceful just like his environment. He comes back to his camp, throws a blanket around him and pours a cup of tea. His cup is a found cup. A once high-class cup someone has lost or thrown away. Sam takes the cup of tea and crawls into his shelter. Takes a book from his improvised library, a shelf made of boards and rocks. The shelf has about eight or ten books on it. Sam picks one and starts to read. Suddenly the shelter is knocked down. Two teenagers have started to destroy it. The young boys are high on drugs, not foggy drugs. Razor-edge drugs, violent boys. Sam stands and walks over to one of the boys and looks into his glassy face. Sam's face is about five centimeters from the boy's face. Sam screams,

"Get out of here. Get the fuck out of here."
From behind, the other boy hits Sam on the head. The blow does nothing to Sam. He screams.

"Get the fuck out of here!"

The boys are sobered by the sound of Sam's energy. They move away from him. Sam screams again. "Go, go, now!" The boys go down the beach throwing Sam the finger—but from a safe distance. Sam replaces the driftwood and puts the blanket over the frame. He finds his book and continues to read. He says quietly:

"I wish people would leave me alone, God damnit. Damnit."

Later in the day, Sam takes a walk down the beach. He is going to pick up some provisions from a small grocery store about a kilometer away. The sea is calm now. In the distance Sam sees a family having a day at the beach, a young man lying in the sun, woman under an umbrella and young boy playing in the water. Sam comes nearer and nearer. He walks through them without looking at them. They ignore him.

Sam comes to a simple building on the beach, a grocery store. He goes inside. He picks out a few items and brings them to the counter. A heavy woman is behind the counter.

"That be all, Mister?"

Sam nods. The woman rings up the bill.

"That'd be 640 francs."

Sam takes the money from his pocket and lays it on the counter. The woman takes the money.

"Another few weeks most of the summer people are gone. The sea's gettin' rougher. Wouldn't catch me in that damned water. Let the damned surfers have it."

Sam goes out the door. He starts towards the water.

The woman calls out,

"Hey Mister, winter here is cold and there ain't no people around. People like you, live like you do, live rough, better head south. There ain't no people here in winter."

She goes inside. Sam watches her deliver her message, probably done with good intention, then he turns around and walks towards his camp about a kilometer away. In the distance, he sees a crowd of people where the family was. He sees an ambulance, parked near the umbrella. He comes nearer. The crowd has backed away from the ambulance. The survivors are being cared for by two men and a woman wearing white coats. Almost inconspicuously there is a body lying on the flat sand covered by a sheet. The body is lying on its back, a little hand is sticking out from under the sheet. Sam walks through the catastrophe. He gets about 30 meters beyond it.

He screams.

"God, don't follow me! Leave me alone! You are following me!

Sam reaches his camp. The wind has picked up. All the greens have turned to grey. The waves are moving closer to the camp, closer than they normally do. Sam puts his provisions in his shelter and turns to deal with this thing, this sea, this next confrontation. The wind becomes rain and wind. The sky blackens with the oncoming night and claims the privilege, the right, to frighten, to terrify. Having killed the child, the sea now looks for new blood. First it swallows the sun and then turns to Sam. The sea's grey breath has blown Sam's shelter down the beach. Sam goes to a high place ready to do battle with any and every element hell's mind could conjure. Thunder cracks through the battleground. Wind lifts everything that is not rooted in hell's ass. Magic holds Sam to the earth.

He screams,

"God! Why are You following me?! What do You want?! Leave me alone. Let me leave You alone! Where are You driving me!!! I AM insane!! What more do You want?!!"

All through Sam's speech the heavens and the earth explode in their most violent language.

He continues to rave.

"I WANT NOTHING FROM YOU! PLEASE... WANT NOTHING FROM ME!"

Sam falls exhausted into the black sea.

He wakes the next morning. He is lying on the flat beach. The tide has retreated. It was as if the sea had never left its bed. Sam lies on the beach like a twisted piece of rag. The sun is high. He opens his eyes and sees white light. At first it does not hurt—then it does. He jerks up.

"Where did you go, you son of a bitch?"

He looks at the quiet, innocent sea. He walks to where his shelter had been. There is hardly a trace of it left.

"So, this is also not my element. Does a person without a system have an element?"

Sam walks away from the sea into a meadow. On the other side of the meadow is a road which leads to a highway, which leads to houses and buildings and tall chimneys that pour human by-products into a discussion which does not allow the question, 'What are we doing to Eden?' Sam's mind moves into the bottom of a 'Game Boy' picture of reality. He becomes a human dot. The little human dot moves into the playing-field and changes into a non-human dot that makes funny sounds as it goes from left to right.

###############

Sam crawled back to Antwerp. There was some money left, residuals from plays, but not much. He wandered in the city. One street was as good as another. He felt he was being followed but when he turned around no one was there. When he grew tired, he went to his room with the hot plate. He tried to write, but the grains of words were all looking alike, words in a desert of words. He found safety in giving away his sanity. What had sanity given him? Only a kingdom of illusion, a castle of vapor. Rest was a memory. Sam ends up in his small rented room in Antwerp. He is writing a play. He looks ill. His beard is rough. Eyes tired. He is drinking tea with lemon. Exhausted, he falls onto an unmade bed. Then suddenly, he jumps up from the bed. He grabs his coat and runs out of the room, and into the streets of Antwerp. It is September. Light rain. Sam is cold and sweating. The grey afternoon won't have to change very much to become night. Streetlight and September light in Antwerp after 5 o'clock are about the same thing.

A prostitute, a black woman, very beautiful in a self-made way, blond wig, light jacket that does not obscure the merchandise, stands in a door-way.

"Hey, honey, do you want to go out?"

"Not tonight. Not feeling too good."

She comes out of the doorway.

"I can make you feel good. Give you a good massage."

"I think I got a fever. You don't need a fever, honey."

Sam moves on down the street.

"You are right, darling. I don't need no fever." She goes back to her position in the doorway.

Sam walks down the street. In the distance he sees a lighted sign: 'Chaim's Restaurant'. As he approaches the restaurant, he sees a large black car parked in front of an apartment building. A man with long flowing white hair steps out of the car. He is wearing traditional Chassidic clothes, black suit and white shirt, also a white silk yarmulke. Over the suit he wears a winter coat with a fur collar. The older man notices Sam staring at him. The older man's eyes are kind, very blue and somewhat recognizing. 'Does this man know me?' Sam asks himself. He moves on down the street towards Chaim's restaurant. He enters the restaurant. It is a small restaurant with pictures of r abbis on the walls. It is a strictly kosher restaurant. A short powerful man is standing behind the counter next to the shawarma grill. The man looks like an Italian gangster wearing a yarmulke. There are simple tables. The man comes over to the table where Sam has seated himself. Sam orders.

"Do you have soup?"

The restaurant man nods.

"Yes."

"With kneidlach?" Again the restaurant man nods.

"I'll take some tea with lemon."

The man goes into the kitchen. Sam is alone in the restaurant. Two men come in speaking Russian, one tall, white shirt, black jacket, black pants, the other man short, same clothes. The tall one is wearing a black hat with a short brim. He looks like a comedian, big brown eyes with an alcoholic glow and a very large mouth which moves awkwardly around Russian words. The short man has white hair and is ready to do some serious eating and drinking. They both nod to Sam. The waiter brings Sam's soup and brings the two men a bottle of Jack Daniels and some lemons. He takes their order and goes into the kitchen. The older man pours two drinks, cuts a lemon in a half, and squeezes the juice into the bourbon. They raise the glasses, say the blessing for booze, nod to Sam and begin an evening that probably had already begun anyway.

As Sam eats his soup, a family comes in, a young man and woman both in Chassidic dress, and three children. They all nod hello to Sam. In comes the diamond man, a heavy man, very black hair, black beard, black pants and jacket, white shirt, talking on his mobile phone the whole time. The diamond man nods hello to Sam. The two Russian drinkers continue to eat and drink. There are many lemon halves on the table and the bottle is less than half full. The mandatory prayer before each toast has become more and more serious and more and more muddled. After each toast the men nod to Sam. Sam is confused. He begins to feel embarrassed at the attention he is receiving from all these strangers.

Sam hears a small voice say 'Shalom Schmuel' (Hello Sam). He turns and looks for the speaker. There is no one next to him, only a picture of a famous bearded rabbi on the wall. 'Shalom Schmuel' he hears again. He looks at the picture. 'Shalom Schmuel'. The lips on the picture move.

"What the fuck!"

He stands and goes to pay his bill. The restaurant man takes his money and says, "Shalom Schmuel".

Sam is astonished.

"Do I know you?" The restaurant man smiles. Sam turns and starts out the door. The whole restaurant suddenly looks at Sam and shouts "Shalom Schmuel". He runs out the door. People on the other side of the street turn and say: "Shalom Schmuel". Sam spins around and sees his reflection in the restaurant window. He is wearing Chassidic clothes. He has payes, 'the curls around the ears' and the yarmulke and a black hat over the yarmulke, black coat, etc. Startled, he gasps, "My God!" He starts to run. Chassidic people begin to come out of nowhere. "Shalom Schmuel". He looks down the street and sees some Chassidic men dancing in a Broadway musical style towards him, singing "Shalom Schmuel". He runs away down the street. He sees a porno shop a few blocks away and runs inside. He is inside the shop in his Chassidic clothes looking out the entrance door to see if anyone is following. When decides he is safe, he relaxes, and turns around to see the customers of the store staring at him. He goes over to the patron of the store, a fat powerful—but mainly fat—man. He asks cautiously,

"Do you know me?"

"Never saw you before in my life, pal."

"Thank God!"

The customers have resumed their browsing and Sam picks up a sex magazine with one eye looking out of the door of the shop. He begins to look at the pictures in the sex magazine and suddenly screams. The photos are of Auschwitz victims. Bodies piled up. Sam screams and finds himself in bed. He has dreamed this whole nightmare.

##############

The few threads of sanity that hold his shattered mind together are coming undone. He jumps out of the bed and looks at himself in the mirror. He goes to the sink and rinses his face. He grabs his coat and runs down the stairs and outside. It is midday, bright sun. He is bewildered; he has slept about 15 hours. He looks where the prostitute was and the doorway is empty. He runs toward the Chassidic neighborhood, he cautiously enters the neighborhood and stands across the street from a synagogue. A member of the congregation is coming out of the synagogue for a break between prayers. His eyes are rich with patience, pain and love. His name is Chaim.

"Why do you stand here? Are you a Jew?"
Sam grimaces.

"Oh God, not that again."

"Are you a Jew?"

"Yes! Yes!"

"Come to the Shul. Today is Yom Kippur."

"Go to hell!"

"Come to the Schul."

Two members of the congregation come over.

"Chaim, er ist meshugge. Lass ihn."

The second man takes Chaim's arm.

"What do you need this for? He is crazy,"

Chiam speaks gently.

"Ich komme gleich. I'll join you in a

second."

The men walk away. Again Chaim speaks to Sam.

"Come in the Shul."

Sam looks at Chaim with disgust.

"Look at you. Do you even know how

stupid you look?"

Chaim answers gently.

"How should I look? I should look wise?

Complete? The finished product? I look like what I am, the

smallest part of the smallest part of God."

Sam shouts.

"Leave me alone!"

"Are you afraid?"

"Afraid to be a fool, yes."

"Be a fool. Leave being wise for those who have finished learning."

"I'll come to your Shul. Today is Yom Kippur. OK, I'll come eating a hotdog. You think I won't? So, Mr. Rabbi, I'll eat a hotdog in your Shul."

Chaim motions to a young man who is watching the conversation.

"Geh zum Bahnhof. Get a hotdog, bring it here."

The young man is surprised.

"Rabbi, are you crazy? Bist Du meshugge?"

Chaim looks patiently at the young man.

"Pikuach nefesh. To save a life."

The young man runs to the hotdog stand. Sam yells at Chaim, trying to provoke him.

"Do you think I won't, you clown? You think I won't?!!"

Chaim looks at him and waits. The young man returns with the hotdog and gives it to Chaim. He takes it and gives it to Sam. Again Sam tries to provoke Chaim, tries to force him to say 'Get out of here!' but Chaim gently and patiently waits till Sam's anger is discharged. He sees the pain and torment that lie just under the surface. Finally Sam resigns. He says in a flat voice,

"Let's go."

They enter the synagogue and the congregation stares unbelievingly at Sam. He is eating a hotdog on the holiest day of the Jewish year, a day of fasting and praying. Sam snarls.

"So let's start the service. You want a bite? You must be hungry."

The voice of a young cantor begins the afternoon prayer. Suddenly, Sam freezes. He drops the hotdog and runs to the bima. The congregation stares in disbelief as Sam grabs the young cantor by the arm and pulls the sleeve up to show a tattoo. The young cantor is Yitzchak.

Yitzchak cries, "Papa!"

Sam stares at his son.

An elderly man comes out of the congregation and steps up to the bima. Yitzchak's stepfather has grown golden in age. His hair and beard have turned to cream. His eyes are soft. He stands between Sam and Yitzchak and rests his gentle hands on their shoulders. He becomes a bridge of love between two islands once separated by seas of despair, now joined in the pool of light pouring through the windows of the synagogue.

There is a light that exists in the clouds which envelop the earth, a light which swirls and dives into the caves of these clouds. This light finds its way into the most hidden, most secret crannies of darkness. A piece of this light shines in the faces of a father and a son.

THE HOLE IN THE HEART

The Play

CHARACTERS

Sam Levine, Holocaust survivor

Yitzchak, his son

German soldier

GI

Cantor

16 members of congregation

Adib, theater director

Actress

Annika, journalist

Jimmy, member of P.A.L. club

Social worker

1st desk man at medical center

2nd desk man at medical center

1

Dawn. Pit filled with dying and dead bodies.

Music over: 'Adagio' by Samuel Barber.

Sam is about twenty-three. He is wearing dirty pants, no shirt, no shoes. He is carrying his three-year-old son, Yitzchak, in his arms. Yitzchak is holding on to his father, his arms around his father's neck. They both have numbers tattooed onto their arms. They are being led up to the top of a dirt hill by a German soldier carrying a rifle. The soldier places Sam and Yitzchak in position at the top of the hill. Then he steps back about three meters. He raises his rifle and aims at Sam's back.

After a few seconds, about six, the soldier fires and Sam and Yitzchak fall down the hill, into the pit. They are separated from each other by the fall. The soldier glances down from the dirt hill, then turns and leaves the stage. There are several seconds of silence, an eternity, then Yitzchak comes to. It is dark. He gets to his feet and looks for his father. He can't find him in the dark. Yitzchak leaves the stage calling "Papa! Papa!" Eventually Sam comes to. His back and his left shoulder are bleeding. The bullet had passed through Sam's back and came out through his left shoulder. Sam mumbles, "Yitzchak... Yitzchak" and crawls up the dirt hill. Sam exits. Yitzchak cautiously re-enters and crawls into a corner of the stage. A GI comes from the audience and up onto the stage. He is wearing full battle gear. He is carrying a rifle. The GI is tense, ready to kill whatever moves. He notices Yitzchak curled up in a corner. Yitzchak is trembling with fear. The GI goes to Yitzchak. He whispers, "It's OK. It's OK." The GI lays his rifle down and removes his coat.

He gently wraps his coat round Yitzchak.

Music fades out

2

Yitzchak is now twelve years old. He is with his adoptive father, a cantor, the head of a religious family in Antwerp. It is Shabbos afternoon. The two are sitting under a tree outside the synagogue. The cantor is preparing Yitzchak for his Bar Mitzvah. Without being aware of it, Yitzchak pulls a leaf from the tree.

CANTOR: Yitzchak, today is Shabbos, you shouldn't take a leaf from the tree.

YITZCHAK: Why not? It's just a leaf.

CANTOR: When you take the leaf from a tree, it kills the leaf. It's like taking a child from its family.

YITZCHAK: (*looks at the leaf in his hand*) I was taken from my family and I didn't die.

CANTOR: Baruch Shem (Thank God).

YITZCHAK: You see, we leaves are not so fragile.

CANTOR: Some leaves are and some aren't.

YITZCHAK: I'm a strong leaf.

CANTOR: Baruch Shem.

YITZCHAK: *(gently putting the leaf on the ground)* Why are some people strong and some not? Was my father strong?

CANTOR: He was very strong. To have a son like you, he must have been a giant of a man, a soul as strong as a lion.

YITZCHAK: I remember him holding me. We were standing near a ditch, standing on a pile of dirt. He held me very tight, then we fell. That's all I can remember. My mother was strong, too. She used to sing to me. Her voice was very low. I will

be Bar Mitzvah in a few weeks. I will be a man. I

will be a tree like that one *(he points to a small tree)*

Not a big tree, but I won't be a leaf any

more. Do you believe in God?

CANTOR: Do you?

YITZCHAK: It's Shabbos. I must be honest.

CANTOR: Be honest.

YITZCHAK: If there were a God with a long white

beard, would all those horrible things… there is no

God. God is an invention in the Torah.

CANTOR: For me God is a feeling. God is a warm

feeling that holds the world together.

YITZCHAK: But God doesn't make sense.

CANTOR: No, Yitzchak. God doesn't make sense. Maybe it's not important that God makes sense.

YITZCHAK: *(looking seriously into the cantor's face)* But things have to make sense. I will soon be a man and I want to know what I'm supposed to do. My father would want me to find his killer and to kill him. My mother, too. I can't just do nothing. Not as a man. As a boy I could—but not as a man.

CANTOR: *(gently takes the boy's face in his hands)* In a few weeks, you will give your Bar Mitzvah. There will be many people listening to you, many people who have memories like you. Many who would take a gun in their hand instead of a siddur. But every prayer that you sing, every law, every rule in our religion has one purpose and only one purpose, to show the highest respect and love for life. If we don't love life, then what is the tragedy of a loss of life? You are young, maybe one day your questions will be answered. But I think I know what your mother and your father would really want. They would want you to leave death behind. They would want you to live, to receive the love they wanted to give you. To receive love and then to give love, that's our purpose in life. That's the order we yearn for. And there is one more thing I must tell you, one more thing I want you to know. I love you, Yitzchak, I love you.

The cantor puts his arms around Yitzchak. The cantor and Yitzchak exit.

3

Synagogue. A platform CS, behind the platform a Star of David.

Eight women enter from SR and eight men enter from SL. The men are wearing prayer shawls and yarmulkes. The women are dressed for attending religious services. Their heads are covered. The men and the women are separated by the platform. They comprise the congregation.

Young Yitzchak enters wearing a white silk robe and a white silk yarmulke. He is holding a prayer book. Yitzchak is followed by the cantor. Yitzchak mounts the platform. The cantor remains standing on the floor. Yitzchak glances at the cantor, opens his prayer book and sings 'Shochanad moro ve koddosh shemo'. The congregation repeats what Yitzchak has sung and Yitzchak's Bar Mitzvah has begun.

4

Theater in Israel. Older Sam. Adib.

Adib and Sam are in a small theater in Jaffa. There is a sign on the side of the stage, which reads, 'Jaffa Theater presents REAL ESTATE by Samuel Levine. Premiere Thursday, March 28, 8 pm.'

Behind Sam and Adib is a platform which represents the stage. At the back of the platform there is a sign which reads 'SHOWER'.

ADIB: We'll start rehearsing in about ten minutes. Sam, do you mind if I ask you a personal question?

SAM: What personal question?

ADIB: It's that tattoo. They can remove it, you know, take it off.

SAM: Don't worry about it.

ADIB: It's none of my business.

SAM: It's a phone number I don't want to forget.

ADIB: It's none of my business. The rehearsals are going well. Do you think people will get it, about the land?

SAM: I don't give a shit if they get it or not. It's what I want to say. That's my job, to say what I want to say, what I think is true. People have been living without my advice for millions of years. They will continue to do so.

ADIB: Then why did you write it, if you don't think it'll change anything? What's the point?

SAM: What's the point of anything? Everything doesn't have to have a point. Life doesn't have a point. It's like God. Does God have a point?

ADIB: Some people think so.

SAM: Some people didn't lose their son, their family. It's easy for some people to believe in points. I write to keep my family alive. They shot my wife, my son, but bullets don't kill, Adib. *(Sam opens his shirt.)* Do you see these bullet wounds? My wife and my son's souls crawled into my chest, and as long as I'm alive, they are alive here in my chest. They are safe here, here inside me. That's why I write, to be alive in spite of everything, in spite of idiots, monsters, everything. I write to stay alive, Adib, alive for my family and for anyone else who doesn't want to accept death. Death doesn't exist, Adib. I wish it did. It would put an end to things. We're stuck. We're in this stupid meaningless life forever. You have all these people in Israel, in Palestine killing each other for land, which will soon be their common restaurant where they will all go, not to eat, but to be eaten. Worms don't bother with details like passports and skin color.

As Sam and Adib talk, people walk onto the platform, men, women and children, all dressed in concentration camp clothes. They stand jammed together, all facing upstage.

ADIB: OK everybody. Let's start the rehearsal.

An actress who has been standing with her back to the audience turns to face the audience.

ACTRESS: Well, dear audience, it's time for me to take the famous shower. You've seen it many times, I'm sure. People screaming, crying. Maybe you'll be able to make my voice out. You know my voice by now. You've been hearing it all night. I think I'll scream in a new way, a way I've never screamed before and never will again. Or is that true? Have I screamed like that before? What do we have now? 1974. I think I screamed in 1840. I was what the Americans call an 'Indian' then. They had the Indian Removal Act. Of course, no showers, no running water. Blood ran. 1940 we don't need to talk about. What about 2040? Will I scream again in 2040? Will you hear me scream in 2040? Some of you might. Some of you might be screaming with me. Or will the Messiah come? Now, that's of course a nice thought. He will come and there will be no need for plays like this one. Excuse me for breaking the illusion. This is a play—no one is really dying. Mothers are not burying their children. No one is really changing from the human wonder into a pile of slime and blood and entrails. We, the intellectuals, wouldn't allow that, would we? Did we? Will we? Well, my friends, back into character. I am about to die. That gives me the freedom to mention a few things. You are all idiots. You are all land-claiming idiots. Real estate idiots. You won't claim the land, ever. The land will claim you. And as for the Messiah, this earth you want to claim is the Messiah. You are not waiting for her. She is waiting for you. Count on it.

Well, it's time. Please excuse me. It's been a lovely

evening.

The actress turns upstage and joins the group

going through the shower door. Music over: the

last part of 'The Survivor of Warsaw' by

Schönberg. The last person goes through the door

as the last chord sounds and the door shuts.

5

Theater in Jaffa. Sam. Annika.

Adib exits, leaving Sam on stage. Enter Annika.

Annika is tall. She has long blond hair and is wearing sunglasses. She carries a bag over her shoulder, which contains a tape-recorder. She is a newspaper reporter. She walks over to Sam.

Annika: I'm Annika Nielson. I watched the rehearsal. You have a powerful play. Do you mind if I ask you some questions? I'm a reporter with the Tel Aviv News.

(Sam looks at her gently, waiting to hear what she would say next.)

Mr. Levine, many citizens of Israel are survivors of the Holocaust. What does your play say about survivors of the Holocaust?

SAM: It says that some didn't survive.

ANNIKA: Mr. Levine, what inspired you to write REAL ESTATE?

SAM: I don't know.

ANNIKA: World peace is a theme, yes, even a dream which dominates our daily lives. Your play expresses this dream. Do you have plans for a new work?

SAM: I don't plan anything. I... I don't plan. Only what happens, happens, then I adjust... if I can, I say or write what happened. The question for me is not what I plan, but why do things happen, good or bad? I just ask that question.

ANNIKA: Jewish and Arabic relations have been very tense lately. Do you think your play portrays the Arabic community correctly?

SAM: There are many different points of view in the Arabic community, even many different communities within the Arabic community. I don't understand the question. Which community?

ANNIKA: I mean political community.

SAM: Politicians are all in the same community. The play doesn't deal with political issues. It deals with tragic stupidity and with our future. It asks the audience if we want to repeat our past or if we want to take humanity in a new direction, maybe one without politicians.

ANNIKA: What do you care about? What is important to you?

SAM: I care about everything. I care about not being seduced into believing in something I don't believe in.

ANNIKA: What don't you believe in?

SAM: Trust.

ANNIKA: You don't trust anything?

SAM: I like early mornings. Early morning is free from weight.

ANNIKA: Do you trust anything else, anything other than early morning?

SAM: I like tea with lemon, a little sugar. It's late. Do you have a family? Is someone waiting for you?

ANNIKA: I have a daughter, six. She's with her father tonight.

SAM: You're divorced?

ANNIKA: We were never married.

SAM: How long were you not married?

ANNIKA: About seven years.

SAM: Writers are too curious. We ask too many questions.

ANNIKA: Fair is fair.

SAM: Do you love him?

ANNIKA: No. I used to. I had a caesarean. The scar was swollen for a long time. I was fat after the birth. He made fun of me. He forced me one night. It hurt a lot. I didn't love him after that.

SAM: But you stayed with him.

ANNIKA: For the child.

SAM: For the child?

ANNIKA: He could also be very nice. He had his character. Everybody has faults.

SAM: You could have left him.

ANNIKA: I'm used to people like him. My parents were always fighting. They separated when I was young, we were young. I have a brother. He is dark, I mean his hair. Black. My brother and my husband, ex-husband, hate each other. My ex once threw a glass of wine at me and my brother hit him in the nose. I'm used to all that. He helps me with the child. He can be very nice.

SAM: Like your father?

ANNIKA: My father was busy with his women and the sea. My brother and I weren't so important, so we made ourselves important. We got slapped for it, but we became important for a while. Sometimes being slapped is a secret form of being loved.

SAM: I never hit my son.

ANNIKA: You have a son?

SAM: I lost him. I never hit him.

ANNIKA: I'm used to it.

SAM: Do you get used to it?

ANNIKA: Sometimes he's nice.

SAM: Isn't that the worst thing that can happen, getting used to it?

Sam and Annika sit on the platform. Annika takes out her small tape-recorder and puts it on the platform between them. She takes her sunglasses off. Her face is bruised and she has a black eye.

ANNIKA: We had a scene last night when I went to pick up my child. He's jealous. Wanted to know why I was late in picking her up.

SAM: My God. Did you call the police?

ANNIKA: It wasn't necessary. He calmed down.

SAM: Why do you stay with him?

ANNIKA: We're supposed to be talking about YOUR life.

SAM: Why do you stay with him?

ANNIKA: He can be nice.

SAM: Hitler was nice to his dogs.

ANNIKA: Why is it important to you?

SAM: I hate tyrants.

ANNIKA: I appreciate your concern, but I want to talk about you, your life.

SAM: We ARE talking about my life.

ANNIKA: You said you lost your son.

SAM: A tyrant killed him.

ANNIKA: Your wife?

SAM: Also.

ANNIKA: I'm sorry. Maybe you don't want to talk about it. We don't have to.

SAM: That's the point. We DO have to talk about it. If you want to talk about me, my life, then we have to talk about what I will do with the rest of it. You are just as much a victim as my family was. You are a victim of yourself. You have the choice they didn't have. You can leave. They couldn't. If you don't leave, you become one of them. You become the tyrant. I don't cooperate with tyrants. I think our interview is over.

ANNIKA: Wait, Mr. Levine. Please. It's not so simple. Things are not always black or white. If I leave him, he will turn my child against me.

SAM: If you don't leave, YOU will turn your child against you. You will teach your child resignation, even cruelty. You'll teach your child to take the side of evil, to not have any belief in human values, only in the power of force. Your friend, or whatever he is, is sick and so are you. But you can change the course of your child's future and your own future. That's the meaning of my life, the life you want to write about, to change the direction people are going in.

ANNIKA: You can write. You can reach people. I can help you.

SAM: You? You can't even help yourself. You willingly live with a fascist and you want to help me.

ANNIKA: I don't live with him.

SAM: You don't stop him from abusing you. You could call the police. You could put a restraining order against him. Do you enjoy it?

ANNIKA: Excuse me?

SAM: Do you enjoy being hit and abused? Why didn't you report him to the police?

ANNIKA: I have reported him. He doesn't do it so often now, I need him to help me with our child. I can't work and take care of her without help.

SAM: Then get help from someone who isn't a fascist. Other mothers do, single mothers.

ANNIKA: I don't want her to grow up without her father. I did and I can tell you, it's not nice.

SAM: You call a man who hits his wife a father? Does he hit the child?

ANNIKA: Of course not.

SAM: It's a question of time, Annika. It's a question of time. When she is older and has her own mind, she'll learn what you learned, that attention comes in the form of abuse. He loves her enough to hit her. It 'hurts him more than it hurts her, it's for her own good.' Bullshit! She'll expect abuse from her partner just like you do. She'll even do things to make him abuse her, just like you do.

ANN: You said he's jealous. You knew he would be angry if you came late to pick her up.

ANNIKA: Excuse me. I have a right to do my work. Sometimes I work late.

SAM: I know that, but you don't have his permission to be late.

ANNIKA: I don't NEED his permission.

SAM: Tell HIM that. Tell him and he will knock the hell out of you, and you KNOW it. And you WANT it. Otherwise you would tell him to go to hell. Take your child and tell him to drop dead. Believe me, I know women who wouldn't stand for the way you are treated for one second. Annika, you want to be abused. You have a choice millions of women who are rotting under the ground didn't have. You CHOOSE to stay with a monster who is sometimes nice.

ANNIKA: Mr. Levine, please.

SAM: Get rid of him or get lost.

ANNIKA: I only want to help you.

SAM: The Nazis told the people they put in concentration camps that they were doing it for their own good, to protect them. That's what they told them. Then they slaughtered them. You are either with them or against them, black or white.

Dead people aren't in a gray zone. Your help is a killing help.

ANNIKA: Mr. Levine, you're paranoid!

SAM: Thank God! Being healthy on your terms is horrible. I'm leaving, Annika. I know why I live like I do. It's because of people like you, normal people who accept being the victims of dictators, politicians, people who learned in their childhood to get used to it, people who don't have the will or the courage to break the chain of abuse.

Sam exits.

6

Community Center. Yitzchak, Jimmy, 2nd social

worker.

It is twenty years later. Yitzchak is a social

worker. He is sitting behind a desk CS with a

phone on it. Yitzchak's sleeves are rolled up. He

has a tattoo on his arm. The large room is filled

with teenagers from around ten years to twenty

years old. Boys, girls, all colors and sizes,

pantomiming, playing pool, talking, playing ping-

pong etc.

Jimmy runs into the room. He is around fourteen

years old. He is black. His hand is bleeding. He

runs over to Yitzchak. Yitzchak stands up.

YITZCHAK: Hey, Jimmy, what happened?

JIMMY: Fucking asshole chasing me!

YITZCHAK: What happened? Let me see your hand. Come here, Jimmy!

JIMMY: Son of a bitch.

YITZCHAK: Let me see your hand. Man, you got a bad cut there. Let's see it.

Yitzchak takes out first aid equipment and bandages from his desk and cleans the boy's hand. Jimmy bravely suffers the disinfectant.

JIMMY: I fucking destroyed the bastard's truck. Man, he was pissed off.

YITZCHAK: You're gonna need a butterfly stitch.

JIMMY: What the fuck is that?

YITZCHAK: They're gonna have to stitch your hand. Jimmy, don't say fuck all the time.

JIMMY: Hey, listen, Numbers, ain't nobody gonna sew me.

2ND SOCIAL WORKER: *(sticks his head into the office) Izzy, you got a call on three. I think it's from overseas.*

YITZCHAK: Got it. *(Picks up the phone, still holding Jimmy)* Just cool it, Jimmy. *(Into the phone)* Mom, it's great to hear you. Everything all right? Mom, you got me at a bad time. Can I call you back? Right, call you later.

JIMMY: Was that your mom? Hey, Numbers, you told me you didn't have a mom.

YITZCHAK: That was my stepmother. Look, we've got to get you to a hospital.

JIMMY: She live around here? In the neighborhood?

YITZCHAK: My step-family lives in Belgium, a town called Antwerp.

JIMMY: What are you doing here if your family lives in... what do you say?

YITZCHAK: Antwerp.

JIMMY: Right, Antwerp. What are you doing here if your mother lives in Antwerp?

YITZCHAK: I'll tell you the story of my life later. Let's get this here fixed up.

JIMMY: *(starts to go again)* My ass. I ain't goin' to no hospital.

YITZCHAK: *(grabs him)* You want to lose your hand? You want to lose your hand, man? I mean, this is dangerous shit. They might cut your hand off if we don't get this sewed up.

JIMMY: You shittin' me?

YITZCHAK: Do I sound like I'm shittin' you? Let's go.

Jimmy and Yitzchak exit the stage and the teenagers exit also.

Hospital. Jimmy, Yitzchak, first desk man, second desk man, waiting patients.

Large room, desk CS. On the desk is a sign: ST. ANTOINE'S HOSPITAL. The first desk man is seated behind the desk.

Waiting patients enter, some on crutches, others wearing casts on their arms. Jimmy and Yitzchak enter and walk over to the desk. Yitzchak speaks to the man at the desk.

YITZCHAK: I'm a social worker and this young man has cut his hand. He needs a butterfly stitch, I think.

DESK MAN: *(not looking up from his desk)* Fill this out, please. Are his parents here?

YITZCHAK: He doesn't have any parents.

DESK MAN: Someone from his family has to sign this.

YITZCHAK: The boy doesn't have any family. Please just stitch him up.

DESK MAN: I'm sorry, we can't administer to him without family consent.

YITZCHAK: *(hits the desk with his fist)* Cut the shit, just stitch him up.

DESK MAN: *(looking up with a face that was better when he was looking down)* I'm sorry. We can't.

Yitzchak and Jimmy turn.

JIMMY: What's with this fucking hospital?

YITZCHAK: Don't worry, Jimmy, there are other hospitals. Jimmy, you gotta quit saying fucking all the time.

They exit. The first desk man exits, carrying the St. Antoine's Hospital sign with him. The second desk man enters, carrying a St. James' Hospital sign, which he places on the desk. Jimmy and

Yitzchak enter and go to the desk.

YITZCHAK: Hello, I'm a social worker and my
friend here needs his hand stitched.

SECOND DESK MAN: Please fill out this form.
We will need family consent.

YITZCHAK: I'll sign.

SECOND DESK MAN: Are you a member of his
family?

YITZCHAK: I'm his fucking uncle!

7

*Yitzchak's studio. Posters of Hebrew letters on
the walls. An easel with a painting of the letter
Aleph (A) on it. The painting is 'prepared', i.e. a
stage technician is standing behind the painting
with a hypodermic needle filled with 'blood'. On
cue, he will squirt the 'blood' through the
painting from behind.*

*Yitzchak is alone on the stage. He has a knife in
his hand as he glances at the painting of the
Hebrew letter. (Cue stagehand) A dark red color
appears to be dripping from the top of the letter,
then it seeps out of the letter. The color begins to
run down the painting. Yitzchak isn't frightened
by what he sees. He walks over to the painting*

and looks closely at the moving color. Soon the whole painting is dripping red paint. The color is running into the white area round the letter. Yitzchak pushes the point of his knife into the wrist of his free arm, the arm with the number on it. His arm begins to bleed. Yitzchak watches the red blood come out of his arm. At first the blood comes out slowly. Yitzchak pushes the point of the knife deeper into his arm and the blood comes out faster. Soon it is pulsing out of his arm to the rhythm of his heartbeat. He places the bloody side of his arm onto the painting. Yitzchak loses consciousness and falls to the floor. Enter cantor.

The cantor wraps Yitzchak's arm. He sits down next to Yitzchak. Yitzchak is lying on the floor. He comes to.

YITZCHAK: Blood is life and the letter was dead without my blood. I wanted to give it life, all the dead letters in my paintings must be brought back to life, otherwise they'll just lie there like corpses in a ditch, millions of corpses.

CANTOR: You can't bring the corpses back to life.

YITZCHAK: Papa, there's something wrong with me. I saw the letters bleed. They started to bleed. I really think I'm going crazy or something.

CANTOR: I'm sure it's connected to your past, when you were a little boy, in that horrible camp with your dad. It's understandable that that

horrible time in your life would leave its marks.

Do you remember your father? Can you

remember what he looked like?

YITZCHAK: No. I probably look like him.

CANTOR: Do you think he survived?

YITZCHAK: Everybody was killed, shot. They

all died.

CANTOR: You didn't die.

YITZCHAK: Sometimes I wish I had.

CANTOR: Do you feel guilty that you didn't die?

YITZCHAK: Why should I feel guilty? I didn't

do anything. I was just a kid. I didn't do anything.

I was just a kid! A little boy! I didn't do anything.

(Tears and anguish flood into his face.) I was just a little kid.

CANTOR: If your paintings start moving again, call me. Night or day, call me. Is it a deal?

YITZCHAK: Do you think he is still alive?

CANTOR: I'll answer you in a very unprofessional way. Only God know if your father is alive. Only God knows.

YITZCHAK: Papa, why do people hurt each other? Why do we hurt ourselves? Why do people not love each other?

CANTOR: Yitzchak, when will we hear your voice again in the synagogue? When will you sing the services again?

YITZCHAK: I think I've forgotten how

everything goes.

CANTOR: I'll help you remember.

8

Street in Antwerp near the synagogue.

Thunderstorm. Sam is wandering in the street. He

is lost both physically and mentally. His clothes

are in tatters. He looks like a homeless bum. Rain

and thunder interrupt his speech, as if to give a

celestial answer to his questions. He screams.

SAM: God! Why are You following me? What do

You want? Leave me alone. Let me leave You

alone! Where are You driving me? I AM insane

already! What more do you want?!

(All through Sam's speech the heavens and earth

explode in their most violent language. He

continues to rave.) I WANT NOTHING FROM

YOU! PLEASE... WANT NOTHING FROM

ME!!! *(He wanders in front of the synagogue. The cantor comes out of the synagogue.)*

CANTOR: Why are you standing here? Are you a Jew?

SAM: Yes! Yes!

CANTOR: Come to the Schul. Today is Yom Kippur.

SAM: Go to hell!

CANTOR: Come to the Schul.

SAM: *(looking at the cantor with disgust.)* Look at you. Do you even know how stupid you look?

CANTOR: *(gently)* How should I look? I should look wise? Complete? The finished product? I look like what I am, the smallest part of the smallest part of God.

SAM: Leave me alone!

CANTOR: Are you afraid?

SAM: Afraid to be a fool, yes.

CANTOR: Be a fool. Leave being wise for those
who have finished learning.

SAM: I'll come to your Schul. Today is Yom
Kippur. OK, I'll come, dressed like I am.

*(The cantor gently and patiently waits till Sam's
anger is discharged. He sees the pain and torment
That lies just under the surface. Finally Sam
resigns. He speaks in a flat voice.)* OK, let's go.
*Inside the synagogue. Sam, Yitzchak, cantor.
There is a platform CS. Behind the platform is the
Star of David. As Sam and the cantor enter the
synagogue, Yitzchak, dressed in a white silk robe*

and wearing a white yarmulke, comes up to the

platform. He is holding a prayer book. He doesn't

notice the cantor or Sam. Yitzchak begins to sing

the Yisgadal prayer. Suddenly, Sam freezes. He

runs up onto the platform and grabs the young

cantor by the arm and pulls the sleeve up to show

a tattoo.

YITZCHAK: Papa!

Sam stares at his son. The cantor steps up to the

platform. Yitzchak's stepfather has grown golden

in age. His hair and beard have turned to cream.

His eyes are soft. He stands between Sam and

Yitzchak and rests his gentle hands on their

shoulders. He becomes a bridge of love between

two islands once separated by seas of despair,

now joined in the pool of light pouring through

the windows of the synagogue. Curtain.

Lightning Source UK Ltd.
Milton Keynes UK
UKHW021458130422
401513UK00006B/214